DO NO
HARM

DO NO HARM

MARY M. MCNAUGHTON

Printed in the United States of America

Library of Congress Control Number: 2018944927
ISBN: Softcover   978-1-64376-002-5
         eBook   978-1-64376-003-2

Published Date: 06/2018

To order copies of this book, contact:

PageTurner, Press and Media
601 E., Palomar St., Suite C-478, Chula Vista, CA 91911
Phone: 1-888-447-9651
Fax: 1-619-632-6328
Email: order@pageturner.us
www.pageturner.us

CONTENTS

DEDICATION

This book is dedicated to all those who have lost a child due to
accident or illness, their lives snatched away in a blink
And
In loving memory of my daughter, Gina May McNaughton, in
gratitude for the gifts of love she gave to me
And
To my many friends

ACKNOWLEDGEMENTS

Thanks to Mary Ann Waller, who not only edited my novel but also gave me greater knowledge about literary writing. I'm particularly grateful to Pam Farrell, who took the time to review and discuss ideas and offered invaluable suggestions. My appreciation goes to Douglas McNaughton, my son, and to my many friends who kept faith in me and encouraged me to keep writing when I ran into roadblocks. Thanks to Mark Malatesta, my coach, who provided me with general guidance about the publishing industry.

CHAPTER ONE

Defeated and afraid, she continues to lay motionless, dirt and leaves on her mouth, until she is almost certain he's gone. Then she rolls over, feels the cold, wet ground on her back and stares at the sky. Finally, shaking, she finds her purse and takes her pocket knife out of it. She waits for him to come back.

Chaos swirled in Jessica's mind as she looked into the mirror. Purple circles beneath her eyes advertised how little she had been sleeping. Her cheeks were more lined than they had been three months ago, and her long black hair, once her best feature, now hung in a tangled mess. Her face was too pale, and her lips…well, her lips seemed set in a curl of boundless contempt.

She bent over the sink and scrubbed her face with soap, trying to clean the rancid odor out of her nostrils. The awful smell of him, never forgotten, as though he was still there… Looking back into the mirror, she inhaled deeply and finally forced herself to calm down, to push these vile thoughts from her mind.

She was scheduled to attend an early-morning introductory

session for new surgical residents at the Oregon Health and Science University. Being late wasn't acceptable. She quickly took a shower, dressed in midi-length navy skirt and white cotton blouse, grabbed her jacket and purse from the sofa, and dashed to the car. Speeding up Sam Jackson Park Road, she found herself taking S-curves with excessive speed, even though she realized she wasn't going to be late after all.

When Jessica walked into the hospital's assembly room, she saw groups of male residents in their mid-to-late 20s, all dressed professionally, wearing white coats over trousers, white shirts, and ties. All men were talking and laughing amongst themselves. Heart pounding, stomach queasy, and no longer feeling calm about anything, she nonetheless skillfully made her way through the crowd and seated herself in the back row. Clutching her new, clean notebook, she made sure that her ballpoint pen wasn't leaking ink onto her name tag, which was sewn over the lapel of her white coat. A few men smiled at her, though most frowned or turned their backs. *Dear God, all these men to compete with,* she thought.

Jessica was entering her first of four years in surgical residency. Even in the hospital, with her white lab coat on, she found it hard to believe she'd been accepted for the program. She'd read that just last year, 1974, only a little more than 10 percent of all the general surgeons in the country were women. But she'd wanted to become a doctor since she was 10. Momentarily, she went back to that time: that incredible raw burn on her arm, shoulder area and neck after her aunt had dropped the coffee pot, the trip to the hospital, that wonderfully kind and gentlewoman doctor. To learn to help heal like that! From that time on, she knew what she wanted to be when she grew up. Now, she was determined not just to reach that goal, but to excel in it.

Right now, in this assembly room, the real test of her determination was beginning. She sat up straighter in her chair and her lips almost curled into a small smile.

Everyone stood when Dr. Karl Gunner, professor of surgery, and a hospital board member, walked into the room. The doctor was a large beefy man of 45-50 years wearing a wrinkle-free crisp white coat and shoes polished to a mirror shine. He waved generally at the room and said cordially, "Please sit," then almost immediately commanded, "Everyone sit down." Everyone did.

"Gentlemen…" Dr. Gunner paused, his mouth twisted into a grimace, and focused on Jessica. "Oh, yes, and lady. Welcome." Sarcastic smiles and subtle snickers resonated throughout the classroom.

The doctor launched into his presentation, describing his credentials and the universities from which he'd obtained each degree, placing emphasis on his current status. He half-smiled then, and began to give an overview of the residency, stating that first-year residents needed to rotate through specific specialties during the entirety of that first year. "The emergency room will be your major source of training," he told them, "and the chief surgical resident will make the assignments." Finally, he stated that as residents progressed in seniority, more complex procedures—under supervision —would be included in their studies.

He stopped abruptly, glanced about the room, raked a hand through his hair, and peered through thick, horn-rimmed bifocals. His eyes were magnified by the lenses— irises the color of coal. His voice boomed: "The lady in the back row staring out the window. Your name?"

Everyone in the room turned and stared in silence as Jessica looked up. Her mouth opened, but her throat felt so constricted that no words could come through.

Softly, the resident sitting next to her murmured, "Uh-oh. Here comes trouble."

"Your name, miss?" he barked, pointing a long, stern finger at her.

Jessica cleared her throat, the sound magnified by the silence in the room. She felt heat rising up her cheeks. In a low voice she said, "Jessica Tinker, sir."

All right, Mizz *Thinker,*" he said with a derisive grin. "Tell the class why you want to become a surgeon.

"Well…" She hesitated, her mouth dry.

"*Well*, isn't an answer," he shot back.

A surge of anger swept through her. With gritted teeth she stood, squared her shoulders, and stated firmly, "Surgery is a stimulating, challenging, and rewarding specialty for doctors." Her voice was loud and clear now, even though her heart was pounding and her stomach felt like lead.

"Wow!" he exclaimed enthusiastically, sarcastically. "The young lady found her voice." He paced back and forth behind the podium. "Okay, Dr. Thinker, here's another question. What should a man give his wife if she's complaining of a headache?"

"That's easy, he should-"

"Never mind, Dr. Tinker," retorted Dr. Gunner. "That was a rhetorical question. If a woman complains of a headache, the husband should give her two aspirin, send her to bed, and then follow her upstairs to keep her from getting another one."

Many students laughed, while others shook their heads. Jessica quietly sat down and felt her blood boil.

After the session, some residents gathered in groups while others left to meet with their instructors. Jessica joined a group of three who, for a moment or two, seemed to accept her. But then one of them said, "Dr. Thinker, I hope you're not getting a headache," and the rest of them turned snide smiles in her direction.

She glared at them and stalked off annoyed, determined to ignore their taunts, resolved not to let them dampen the anticipation of her first rotation day.

Hours later, Jessica could not wait for her first rotation to end. She had seen more patients than she cared to count, and she needed some relaxation and quiet time. Once she was able to clock out, she walked to her car and drove straight home.

She arrived at her apartment at 6:30 with an excruciating headache, still thinking about Dr. Gunner's stupid sexist joke. *What an insulting bastard! He wouldn't belittle any male resident this way.*

She hurled her keys on the table, flung her coat and satchel on the sofa, and headed for the kitchen. Without hesitation, she opened the pantry cupboard, reached behind two boxes of cornflakes and pulled out a bottle of Stolichnaya. She reached for a tall glass, dropped in a couple of ice cubes from a tray in the freezer, poured a large amount of vodka over the ice and added a small amount of orange juice. After taking two gulps of the cold drink, she fell into her recliner.

Her last coherent thought that evening was: *will I be able to survive this training for four years?*

CHAPTER TWO

As the days, weeks, and months passed, Jessica came to doubt that surgery was her forte, uncertain whether her body and mind could continue to endure the demands of a four-year residency. She worked 45 hours a week in surgery on a schedule that required her to be available for emergency calls every other night; forty-five hours in surgery plus reams of paperwork to be completed and countless lectures to be attended. It was brutal.

One night, she woke up, heart racing, in surgery just as the operating physician was congratulating her team on successful removal of an inflamed appendix and closing the wound with stitches. *Had I actually been asleep?* It seemed so.

There was the usual recap after that, with suggestions about what could have gone wrong—and though she was asleep, luckily nothing had not—and about what could have been done differently. All she could do was nod her head, say "Yes, yes," and try to stop shaking.

What would have happened if the appendix had ruptured? What would have happened if I had caused that to happen?

On Jessica's first day off after that, she woke up determined to spend the day *not* thinking about being cooped up in the hospital and *not* worrying about her future as a surgeon. She guzzled down half of her favorite breakfast smoothie and was grinning cheerfully by the time she dialed her long-time friend Leslie.

"Hey, Dr. Leslie Snow!" she playfully greeted. Jessica and Leslie had known each other since grade school and had roomed together in college. Now, even though their lives were much different, Jessica still single while Leslie had married and had two children, they kept in touch in almost-weekly phone conversations. This time, however, Leslie insisted that Jessica come to her house for lunch. "Around noon, she said.

"Alright. I'll see you, then," Jessica said. An outing was just what she needed.

She arrived at Leslie's home exactly at noon, lifted the brass knocker and rapped twice. Leslie opened the door almost immediately.

"Hello, Jess! Please come in. Another friend of mine should be arriving shortly." She glanced at her wristwatch and said, "I want you to meet him." Her face was flushed and her speech was more rapid than usual. It seemed to Jessica as though Leslie realized that it was improper to invite a man for lunch, probably a single man, without her husband's knowledge.

Jessica stepped inside. She could smell fresh coffee brewing, filling her friend's kitchen with the warm, heady aroma she looked forward to each time she visited. Leslie led her through the house and into her big kitchen, the two of them navigating through a maze of colorful toys on most of the available surfaces. Jason, 4, and Barbara, a year younger, were chasing each other madly about, the former waving a Raggedy Ann doll over his head. Amid all the cheery commotion, coffee was poured and cookies were served.

As Leslie began to work on lunch, Jessica munched on delicious chocolate chip cookies. She hadn't felt this relaxed in weeks, although it did concern her that her friend might be interested in this other man. *How could any woman who had Alexander Snow, such a handsome, huggable, nice man, even look at another?* she thought.

Leslie and Alex had met while she was attending medical school and he law school. After graduation and marriage, they had planned not to have children until they were well-established. Leslie had gotten pregnant by accident, however, and had left her obstetrical practice. She planned to return to it once the children started kindergarten. Meanwhile, though Alex worked long hours to support his family— and what lawyer doesn't work long hours? — he comes home for dinner every evening. Leslie often talked about him helping her clean up after dinner and reading bedtime stories. They both seemed happy.

The two women discussed Jessica's impression of residency (not a happy subject) and her parents' opinion of her career choice (not a happy subject, either, since her parents' idea of their daughter's path in life hinged on husband and home. Preferably a very handsome husband and a very large home).

Leslie said, "Do you remember last year at the New Year's Eve party when you showed everyone that snapshot of you outside your parents' mansion?"

"So, what about it?" Jessica snapped. She had less than pleasant memories of that party.

"Nothing. It's just that most of the doctors at the party thought you were a mercenary little gold digger. They wondered why you were bothering with medical school when you were going to inherit all that," Leslie replied.

"Well, that's too damn bad." Now Jessica was as tense as she'd been all week. She steered the conversation back to discussing parties the Snows hosted each year. She knew about Leslie's compulsive habit to keep lists of names, addresses, likes and dislikes of guests, and even a notation about each person's lifestyle.

"Leslie, do you always invite the same medical people and their partners to your parties?" Jessica asked nonchalantly.

"Yes. Occasionally a few new ones. Why?"

"Well, you have so many wonderful friends. I'd love to get to know some—even make new friends of my own." She forced a smile and shrugged.

Leslie stood quietly for a moment gazing at Jessica and then said, "As a matter of fact, my husband and I plan to host a party in a couple of weeks. You're invited."

"Will many surgeons and faculty be there?"

"Of course. Don't worry; I won't ask how you're performing in surgery." She chuckled at the annoyed look on Jessica's face. She intended to amuse her.

The grandfather clock struck one while the two women were reminiscing about old times and preparing sandwiches. Not even five minutes later, the doorbell rang. Leslie dropped the bread slices on the breadboard and headed for the foyer. When she opened the door, there stood an eye-catching man.

"Come in, come in, Silas," Leslie said smiling. "I want you to meet a long-time friend of mine."

Silas, his name was, was tall and lanky. He had a strong, intelligent face with bright ebony eyes and sparkling white teeth—framed by a mop of dark-chocolate, curly hair. His skin was dark, in sharp contrast with those teeth. Rather than being captivated by his good looks, however, Jessica felt … cautious? As if she'd known the man somewhere.

Leslie quickly made the introduction. "Jessica, meet Dr. Silas Rolland. Silas, Dr. Jessica Tinker."

"Hello, Jessica," he said, grinning as he extended his hand.

"Hello Silas." Jessica held out her hand, feeling like a dog offering a paw, and from the look on Leslie's face, she might as well have been. Leslie frowned, and with tightened lips stared at Jessica, but a split second later smiled. Jessica wondered if Leslie was jealous, since Silas had stepped up so close to her and was continuing to smile. "Silas, do you come to many of these parties?" She asked.

"No, I don't. Do you?"

Just at that moment Leslie looked directly at Silas and said, "Lunch will be ready soon. Hope you're hungry." She gave his arm a squeeze.

Jessica could hear him carrying on a conversation with Leslie as they made their way to the dining room, but she couldn't seem to pay attention to what was being said.

Well past midnight. It's been a nice party at the Snow residence. She walks to her car—and then without warning, an attacker from behind grabs her and drags her into an area overgrown with scraggly bushes. His hand is on her mouth. She can hardly breathe, certainly can't scream, though she tries. He rips her blouse open, all the buttons flying off. It's as if he's torn her breasts. Desperately, she tries to get free, tries to bring her knees up and kick him in the groin, but the man is muscular, tall, overpowering her. She manages to turn toward him and rip his shirt, and sees on his right shoulder a tattoo of a bald eagle. He has a beard. A mustache. He reeks with alcohol. His hair is dark and greasy. Now she can speak. "Please, let me go," she pleads. Then she screams, repeatedly, "Help! Somebody help me!"

Suddenly, Jessica realized Silas has asked her a question. "You've wondered if I attended many of these parties? Yes, I've attended a few over time." Her voice fades. She remembers the pain. She wants her attacker found. She wants him to feel this pain.

"By the way," says Silas now, "what specialty are you pursuing?"

"Hopefully, neurosurgery." Jessica paused, made herself smile, and added, "Time will tell."

Silas kept focused on her as she spoke about her residency. He shifted his body, leaned against the kitchen wall for comfort, crossed his arms, and continued to pay attention. When she finished, he said, "I'm sure you'll make a great surgeon."

"Glad you think so."

"Yes, I do. Leslie mentioned how energetic and ambitious you are."

"Really? Well, I'll be damned," she said shaking her head.

Leslie called everyone to the table for lunch and reminded her children to sit and eat like grownups. Jessica and Silas sat across from each other. Jessica, hungry now, grabbed a sandwich, took a big bite and asked, "How did you and Leslie meet?"

"We met when I entered residency here in Portland," Silas said.

"I was raised in Kingston, Jamaica, and after high-school graduation I completed my baccalaureate degree and four years of medical school at the University of West Indies in Mona, Jamaica before coming here."

"Do your parents still live in Jamaica?"

"My mother does. My parents divorced when I was young, and my father, of American birth, moved to the United States, leaving us behind." He looked down at his wing tips, swallowed, and shrugged his shoulders. "What about you?"

"My mother and her husband live in Seattle. We visit from time to time."

Conversation ensued, sandwiches dwindled, and the children made their excuses. Leslie got up from her chair, stepped next to Silas, placed her hand on his shoulder, rubbed the back of his neck, and then … slid her hand under his shirt and down his spine! "Silas," she said, "you've come a long way and made a life for yourself." Then she removed her hand, ruffled his hair with her fingers, and went to refill his glass.

Silas was silent. His face flushed, but his eyes remained focused on his sandwich. He seemed calm. Jessica, however, was shocked. This was most definitely not the Leslie she knew. She stood, almost knocking over her chair, and said, "Excuse me, but I must go… a lot of things to do. Leslie, thanks for lunch. Silas, I'm pleased to have met you." She picked up her satchel and, without another word, headed for the door.

Silas stood as quickly, hurried after her and said, "I hope very much to see you again."

She looked at him blankly, said goodbye and left.

CHAPTER THREE

When Jessica arrived back at her apartment, she fell into her recliner, still in shock. Leslie, flirtatious and turning on her charm like a light bulb was surprising, but it was Silas she couldn't figure out. Right in front of her, Leslie had thrown herself at the man, and he had allowed it to happen, saying nothing. *What was this relationship about?*

The next morning, Jessica was on the surgical floor heading down a long corridor to see post-surgical patients. She was completely absorbed in thinking about the feasibility of taking time off from school when she felt a tap on her shoulder. It was Silas in a white hospital coat.

"What are you doing on the surgical floor?" she demanded.

"Just wanted to stop by in the hopes of running into you. Would you like to have a cup of coffee?"

"Well, I have a lot of work to do, and I'm on my way—"

"It'll only take a short while. I promise."

Jessica hesitated, struggling for words, and finally said, "I don't think so. Perhaps another time."

"Please, I need to talk to you about yesterday." He was urgent. His brow was furrowed.

"Well, only if it's quick. I have a very busy schedule."

They walked downstairs to the coffee shop on the first floor. Jessica spotted a table near the window and quickly sat down removing her stethoscope from around her neck and putting it in her coat pocket. Silas followed suit. Several students perched on stools at the counter chatted about various medical topics; nonetheless, Jessica and Silas had the space to themselves. They ordered coffee from a crispy, starched waitress who flashed Silas an appealing smile and a wink. Jessica raised her eyebrows.

She expected Silas would come up with some explanation for his unconscionable behavior immediately. Instead, they talked about trivial things. Silas mentioned that he'd planned on returning to Kingston for a visit at year's end. He wanted to see his mother. He spoke lovingly about her, but never mentioned his father. Changing the subject, he said, "One day soon, I hope to work here with Dr. Seth Diesel in research. The center is being expanded and will be ready for full operation soon. That's my ultimate goal."

She was about to reply when the waitress, still smiling, returned to refill their cups and eyed Silas boldly. Silas shifted in his chair, evidently feeling uncomfortable.

"Anything else, honey?" the waitress asked.

"No, thank you." Jessica made it a point to be the one to answer.

They drank the second cup of coffee. Jessica, frustrated at the time this

14

was taking, started the conversation again by saying, "Weren't you going to tell me something of importance about what happened yesterday?"

He looked at her with those hypnotic eyes and said, "Jessica, I feel embarrassed about the way your friend behaved during lunch. There was no reason for her to put her hands on me like that." He fussed with his tie, looked directly at her and said, "She's never done that to me before."

Wanting to forgive him, but not even sure why she should, Jessica said, "Well Silas, maybe Leslie and her husband are having marital problems." *That still wouldn't excuse what Leslie did*, she thought, but kept that to herself.

"Please don't judge me by what happened," he intoned.

"It's not an issue. Forget it," she said.

For a split second, she thought to ask Silas whether or not it would be wise to take some time away from school, to go somewhere, do something so she could just relax. But she instantly decided it was best to keep that to herself as well. Instead, she diverted the conversation to a more professional topic. "What do you know about Dr. Diesel? What's he like? Rumor has it his ego is a mile long."

"Why are you asking?"

"I'll be doing my rotation in research soon."

Silas's expression remained impassive. He rotated his cup of coffee in the saucer and said, "Seth... Dr. Diesel really is a good man. He enjoys instructing anyone interested in research, but he is the boss. He's tough as nails if anyone oversteps boundaries or doesn't measure up to his expectations."

"Is that okay with you?"

"Absolutely." He hesitated, looked directly at her and said, "But then, I'll be working as a research analyst."

Jessica glanced at her watch and said, "I'm really sorry, but I must go."

Silas paid the bill. As they walked out of the coffee shop, he gripped her shoulder, then smiled and released his hold. "Thanks for having coffee with me," he said, looking at her with his sparkling eyes. "Hopefully, we can do this again very soon."

She was silent, surprised.

"Don't work too hard," he said over his shoulder, and they went in different directions.

"Thanks," was her only acknowledgment, probably too late for him to hear.

Late the following day, Jessica walked into the surgical floor to pick up a medical manual. She noticed Dr. Stout standing at the nurses' station. Dr. Stout lived up to his name: kind, slightly round, and always with a big smile for everyone He was an experienced surgeon.

"Hello Jessica." He looked at her nametag, grinned and said, "Jessica Tinker. I got it right. It seems I often confuse students' names. Anyway, how is your training coming along? Tell me again, what year of residency are you in?"

"I've almost completed my first year," she said cheerfully.

"Excellent."

Just then, the intercom blared, "Code red. Code red in ER."

"Damn, I should be at home with my feet elevated, drinking a glass of wine. Dr. Tinker, please come with me."

In the Emergency Room, Dr. Stout was met by the senior surgery resident on call. "The patient is in Trauma Room Two with multiple stab wounds to the abdomen and chest," the senior resident said. "He arrived by ambulance." Jessica entered the ER with Dr. Stout, and saw blood-soaked clothing and sheets. An intravenous had been started, and the resident had ordered X-rays, CBC, comprehensive metabolic panel, and blood type and cross-match.

"Very good," stated Dr. Stout. What's the BP?"

"It's down to 100 over 68. His respirations are shallow and rapid," the resident replied.

"Dr. Stout nodded. "Increase the fluids." Within 20 minutes, a unit of blood was received and hooked into the IV.

Turning, Dr. Stout said, "Jessica, you will assist me. Let's go."

"But ... but I...."

"There is no time to waste. This patient is hemorrhaging. Now, let's get him to the OR!"

In minutes, Jessica had scrubbed and changed into surgical scrubs. As she donned a mask and cap, she felt a rush of adrenalin. Hurrying into the large operating room amid the rhythmic hum of the machinery, she felt powerful. She walked up next to the patient and placed her fingertips at the side of his neck, feeling for the carotid artery and the pulse. She felt one—slow and faint, but definite. The patient looked like death: his face pasty, his eyes closed, and his breathing shallow. She looked up at the anesthetist, who glared at her and announced to the surgeon, "We're all set, sir."

Jessica felt heat creeping up her face under her mask. She could tell that the anesthetist was not pleased with a first-year resident assisting. Distracting her from the awkwardness of the situation, however, was the arrival of Dr. Max Brown, an experienced thoracic surgeon whom Jessica had met while attending one of his classes. He was already scrubbed, and stood along with Jessica ready to assist.

Dr. Stout glanced at Max and said, "Meet Jessica Tinker, one of our first-year surgery residents. I've asked her to assist under your supervision. He glanced at Jessica over the top of his mask, his eyes crinkling, suppressing a chuckle, as though to reassure her.

"Let's see how she can do," said Max.

The next morning, Dr. Gunner called Jessica into his office. She entered the room with some trepidation and was made to stand there for several long minutes in front of his desk, during which nothing at all was said. Then, the professor looked up at her, his eyes blazing and his mouth in a cruel twist. She winced, but stood her ground. *I haven't done anything wrong. I've been directed to assist by Dr. Stout, and I had done a good job.*

Dr. Gunner stood up, came around from behind his desk, and stepped in front of her. There was rage in his hooded eyes. He looked like a predator ready to strike. "What's this I hear about you doing a complicated, near-death case with Dr Stout. You're not even into your second year," he shouted.

She was terrified. Stepping back, almost falling back, she said, "Sir… Dr. Brown did the surgery with Dr. Stout. I was only of minuscule help." It wasn't true, but it might get her out of this trouble. Ignoring her, Dr. Gunner bellowed, "What the hell do you think you're doing?" He paused for a breath, his face contorted with anger. "God dammit, what were you doing assisting on a near death case?"

Jessica stood facing him, her expression still professional, but now she was simply unable to speak. She turned and walked out of his office.

CHAPTER FOUR

I t was well known in medical circles that Dr. Karl Gunner had built a reputation of being the best in the country in his profession. His thoracic surgery expertise was in demand, and he rarely spent much time away from work. Jessica had heard rumors that both of his wives had divorced him because he was abusive, and that he had become bitter and filled with negative feelings toward women. She understood that he had long ago left his native country, Germany, and became a citizen of United States. She had also learned that he served a brief period of time with the armed forces in Vietnam. She thought about Dr. Gunner all during her drive to work the next morning.

Arriving at the hospital, she immediately went to the nurses' station on the surgical floor, requested the chart for the patient whose surgery she had assisted on, and began reviewing the data. She read the patient's history, which stated that he was a middle-aged Caucasian, recently divorced, who had gotten into a brawl while intoxicated. She read that he had been brought in by ambulance with multiple stab wounds to the chest and abdomen, which she knew already.

As Jessica continued reading, a patient in a wheelchair rolled up silently behind her. Absorbed in her reading, she didn't see him. When she turned to leave the nurses' station, her ankle caught on the wheelchair's foot. She went flying backward, landing squarely in the arms of Dr. Max Brown. He held on to her to keep her from crashing into a cart.

"Are you hurt?" he asked with a half-smile.

"Just my pride. Thank you for rescuing me." Her face felt hot. The nurses and doctors at the nurses' station chuckled. Max removed his arms from around her waist.

One of the doctors standing at the desk remarked, "Good catch."

"I played football in my early college days," Max replied with a laugh. Turning to Jessica, he said, "By the way, Dr. Tinker, I never had an opportunity to let you know that you did one hell of a job assisting Dr. Stout on this patient." He pointed at the chart she was holding. "I was impressed."

"Really?" Jessica's eyes and face lit up. "You thought so?"

"Yes, I did." He stepped closer to her, looked into her eyes, and said, "Would you like to have a cup of coffee?"

"Now?" Jessica said, her eyes wide. The pack of doctors and nurses that surrounded the station paused and waited for her answer.

"If it's convenient."

"Yes, of course," she said, her face flushed, her head and eyes lowered.

Walking side-by-side, Jessica and Max headed for the coffee shop on the first floor. She was conscious of his auburn hair, of his tan and his rugged features. He was considerably taller than her and somewhat older. She felt her heartbeat increase and stomach tighten as she thought about why he might want to have coffee with her.

They sat at a table next to a window. They both ordered coffee, and Max ordered a piece of chocolate cake, which was delivered promptly.

"Are you from this area?" Max asked while enjoying his cake.

"No, my family lives in Seattle, but I attended the University of Oregon at Eugene, and medical school at the University of California, Berkeley. Have you lived here all your life?" she asked.

"All except four years of medical school, four years of residency, four years for board certification, and three years in Vietnam."

"I'd say that makes you an Oregonian." When their eyes met, both laughed for no particular reason. "I understand that Dr. Gunner also did a stint in Vietnam," she said.

"He tells me he served, but I didn't know him, and of course, I'm many years his junior, don't you think?" He laughed.

Jessica could have laughed as well, but suddenly wondered if Max had a tattoo of a bald eagle on his shoulder. That seemed to be her standard reaction these days. Meet a man she liked and then get stopped cold wondering about that tattoo. *I can't rule out anyone as my possible attacker,* she thought, *or at least anyone who might have gone to that party.* It occurred to her to invite Max to go swimming at the city pool. Or play some sport with her that would require him to remove his shirt. Somehow, she had to find out if his shoulder was marked by the bald eagle tattoo.

"It's Jessica, isn't it? May I call you Jessica'?" He was smiling pleasantly, having no idea what she was thinking. There were wrinkles around the outer edges of his eyes. *Eyes that signaled mischief,* she thought."

"Of course."

"Do you mind if I smoke, Jessica?"

Suddenly, she had an idea. She would suggest to Leslie that she hold an autumn party at the Columbia Gorge Hotel in Hood River, Oregon. The hotel is in the heart of a beautiful scenic area and just 50 miles from Portland. Everyone could enjoy the day relaxing and going wind surfing, and she would get to see many of the men who went to Leslie's parties without their shirts on. She closed her eyes, satisfied with the thought.

"Are you all right? Max's voice brought her back from her reverie.

"Yes. I mean, no. No, I don't mind if you smoke, doctor."

"Just Max will do," he said with a frown. He pulled a pack of Camels from his shirt pocket and placed a cigarette between his lips, lit it, and exhaled a plume of smoke at the window. He avoided Jessica's eyes. It's good that you don't smoke. I really need to quit."

They talked for a while about medical issues, and then Max asked, "What motivated you to go into surgery?"

"I'm not really sure. I've known I wanted to be a doctor since I was 10. But a surgeon? Well, I always enjoyed challenges, and surgery seemed like a logical option. What about you?"

"I, too, needed a challenge."

Half an hour later, Max paid their bill, and the two walked out of the coffee shop.

"Thank you for the coffee and the interesting conversation," she said with a smile she hoped was pleasant. Not too business-like in case he was interested personally, but not too friendly in case he wasn't. She didn't know what her interest was. She hadn't been able to get very friendly with anyone since....

"Perhaps we can do this another time." He extended the long, slender fingers of his hand and gave her a firm handshake.

"Sounds good." She smiled and looked him squarely in the eyes. She might be confused, but she could act assured.

* * *

The weekend after Jessica had coffee with Max, she heard again from Silas. He called her at home.

"Hello, Jessica," he said, his deep, resonant voice carrying over the line. "Silas Rolland here. How are you?"

"I'm fine. I know who you are. I recognize your slight Jamaican accent." She laughed, more from nervousness than anything else. There was a momentary silence. Then, "What do you want?" she asked, feeling awkward and lacking in social graces.

"Jessica, perhaps we can go out tomorrow?" He paused. "For dinner? Somewhere nice."

Jessica thought he sounded like a little boy needing attention. "All right, that's a good idea," she said. *An evening out at a nice restaurant would be a treat,* she told herself. And because Silas was Leslie's friend—whatever that might mean—he would probably be a safe date. She knew he could be the one with the tattoo, but he seemed to have this integrity. *Maybe it's those mesmerizing eyes,* she thought.

"I'll pick you up at six," he said, his voice cheerful.

It would be her first real date in more than a year. After she hung up the phone, she went straight to the closet and tried on everything that might do. She decided on a fitted navy dress with a low-cut neckline and a wide red belt and pumps. She would wear her hair in a French twist.

Silas was not there at 6:00 the next evening. He was not there half an hour later, either, after Jessica had had plenty of time to wonder whether he had become involved in a hospital case or had changed his mind about seeing her. Finally, to her surprise and relief, the doorbell rang at 6:40. She opened the door to see Silas dressed in slacks and coffee-colored leather blazer over a cream shirt. His jet-black eyes twinkled.

"I'm glad to see you," Jessica blurted, giving him a quick handshake.

They drove to a restaurant called Andina's. Entering, they were welcomed by a maitre d' and ushered to a quiet corner table. The interior décor was tasteful, Beethoven's Moonlight Sonata playing in the background. The walls were adorned with photographs of the shoreline and of the Adams, Saint Helens, and Hood Mountains.

When the waitress arrived, Silas ordered two Pisco sours, a popular Peruvian drink made with brandy, lemon juice, and sugar. When they arrived, Jessica took a long sip of hers and said, "It's amazing. Tart, strong, refreshing, complex: everything I enjoy." She studied the menu and covertly watched Silas studying her. They both ordered quinoa-crusted scallops which, when they arrived, proved to be enormous and delicious, served over a parsnip and potato puree with wilted spinach. It was a delicious meal followed by another round of Pisco sour and a chocolate mousse with fresh berries.

"Thank you for this delightful dinner and evening. It was an enjoyable experience," Jessica said, and meant it. The sheer decadence of it had brought her completely out of her customary suspicious and nervous state.

"You're so very welcome, Jessie," he responded enthusiastically. His eyes became warm and searching. He leaned closer, "Jessie, I just want you to know that you are beautiful." He gazed at her, then bent his head and whispered, "And you look stunning in that dress. Truly gorgeous." He looked at her as though he were a dog who wants to be petted.

Tears gathered in Jessica's eyes. Silas was the only person who had ever called her Jessie. She lifted her head and stared at him for a moment. "I've been thinking about deferring residency for a few months," she said. She realized that she was directing the conversation away from intimacy, but she continued anyway. "I was thinking about going home for Christmas. I'm tired. I need a rest."

She needed to talk to someone who would understand her. Terrible things had happened to her, things she hadn't told anyone about and would not tell this man until she found out if he was the right person. So, instead, she told him about Dr. Gunner's animosity and bullying, and about the difficulty of being the only female resident among males who would laugh at jokes like the one about the aspirin.

As she talked, Silas sat quietly with his hands clasped and brows furrowed. Then he said, "Jessie, I really don't think you want to defer residency." This was not what she wanted to hear, but she knew Silas was smart and sensitive and probably had good advice. Still, she questioned his motives. *Could he just be self-serving?*

CHAPTER FIVE

S aturday morning at sunrise, Jessica awakened, wandered from her bed to her living room and crawled into her recliner, deep in thought. "You need to reconsider your decision about deferment." Silas's words echoed. She so desperately needed a respite, but to defer schooling would not help find her rapist. She was determined not to give up her search for the man who had done so much harm—she must stay on her mission—but how could she do that while dedicating her whole self to her dream of becoming a surgeon?

"School…. Damn depressing place," she said, though she did realize that her ever-deepening depression was coming from her own dilemma as much as it was from her surroundings. When she had started her residency, she had feared the worst. But she had to admit that when she took part in weekly case presentations, professional staff activities, patient care, and the conferences held by the department of general-surgery, she found most of the program directors and chief residents to be fair-minded. And they were smart and fun to learn from.

Dr. Gunner was the only exception. His hostile behavior toward her was intolerable. At the thought of him, even now safe in her own apartment, she cringed. Gunner reminded her of a Gestapo interrogator in a second-rate World War II movie even when she was awake. When she was asleep, it was Dr. Gunner making sexist jokes in class, all the other students laughing; Dr. Gunner holding her latest paper on high and telling everyone he gave it a failing grade. And the students again laughed. It was nothing short of a nightmare.

She had to get away, escape from these dreams. Disrupting her residency, though, could prove devastating. Would she even be accepted back if she quit now for no reason anybody at the hospital could possibly be aware of? She knew what Gunner would say: "Women. There's no room for women in an operating room. They can't take the pressure, and their patients die because they just can't hack it."

She shook her head in frustration, closed her eyes and sighed. Then without further thought, she stood, walked into the kitchen, opened the cupboard, pulled out a bottle of vodka and mixed herself a drink. She took two swigs, enjoying the taste, then two more gulps. The carefree and relaxed feeling that spread through her body was especially satisfying. *This is much better than coffee,* she thought. She returned to her comfortable recliner, took a few more sips, then quite suddenly decided to go home to Seattle for the weekend.

"Hello?" Her mother's voice was always cheerful on the phone.

"Mother I'm planning to visit you this weekend."

"I'm pleased, honey. Why are you calling so early?"

"I didn't sleep well, so I'm up enjoying a cup of coffee," she lied.

"It's all those hectic hours you work. You really should get more sleep. When do you plan to arrive?"

"Today."

There was a long pause. "Today? When?"

"I'll be there when I can. I'll leave after work."

"I hope you're here before midnight. Don't drive late into the evening. A lot of traffic."

"I'll try my best," and hung up.

After morning rounds, she made arrangements for a resident to cover her weekend shift. Before leaving the hospital, she stopped at the coffee shop for a takeout coffee. Glancing about, she noticed Silas having coffee with another man. She went over to say hello, and Silas stood to greet her.

"I'd like you to meet Dr. Seth Diesel, our chief lab analyst," he said. "Jessie, please sit down." He gestured with his hand toward a chair.

"No, thanks, I'm on my way to Seattle, but it's nice meeting you, Dr. Diesel." She smiled and turned to leave. Silas moved toward her hesitantly, then said, "Jessie, call me soon as you return."

She drove home, packed a few things and began the drive to her parents. She was in turmoil again. *What to do about the nightmares, the fluctuating emotions? Complete the residency or work on finding the rapist? And Silas, Silas as friend or Silas as…?* She wasn't ready, couldn't even think about that. Anyway, what had Leslie's motivation been when she invited Silas to her home and then put on that performance, particularly after telling Jessica she wanted her to meet him? Then Alexander. He was as career-oriented and hardworking as Leslie, and made more than enough money. *Could Leslie want Silas for herself? In addition to her husband? Instead of her husband?*

Mid-afternoon in Seattle in early September was beautiful. A

28

warm, strong wind swept off the sea. Rolling waves echoed like voices in unison, their white crests diminishing as they ebbed from the sandy shore. Jessica parked at Elliot Bay and got out of the car to walk in the sand. She was overcome with loneliness, uncertainty and fatigue. She walked barefoot, digging her toes deep into the sand, all the while trying to unravel her nightmarish past and her worrisome future. She stayed on the beach for several hours, paying attention as late afternoon brought out the soothing blue-gray of the ocean, drawing strength from the immensity of the sea. At least, this visit home would be free of annoyance and pressure, or at least she hoped it would.

The house where Jessica had grown up was a brick edifice with two sturdy redwood columns supporting the entryway. Sweet gums and maples in emerald leaf, a few slightly tipping into gold and amber, framed the house. The shrubbery and flowering plants in the yard were enormous. The entire setting looked like a fantasyland.

She rang the doorbell and then entered, calling out, "Hey, Mother, I'm home." Her mother hugged her, but it was a quick, one-armed affair. She had a faraway look in her eyes that did not disappear even after the two of them had chatted briefly about her drive from Portland.

Jessica, intending to get her mother's view of her dilemma, maybe even get a solution, began with, "Mother, I'm just beginning my second year of residency."

"That's nice," her mother said vaguely. "I hope you're hungry. Earlier, I ordered a gourmet meal, and now I'll call to have it delivered."

Mother served the meal, very tasty and accompanied by cabernet. She took command of the conversation, bombarding Jessica with questions about her social life, her love life, and her residency. Jessica responded as best she could, but she got the impression that Mother was asking out of politeness rather than any real interest, particularly since her daughter had little to report about social events or boyfriends. Jessica's stepfather, Charles, sat in his large, soft-as-dough armchair, sipped his wine, and said nothing, per usual.

As soon as she could, Jessica excused herself and went upstairs to her old bedroom. She sat in the same overstuffed chair she'd had as a teenager and perused medical journals that she'd packed in her satchel. Later, she picked up a Vogue magazine from the bedside table and tried to be interested in the latest styles. A tap on the door was unexpected.

Her mother walked in. "Jessica, what are you doing? You ate dinner, said a dozen words and vanished. Come downstairs and join Charles and me." Her voice penetrated. Her expression was stormy. She marched back down the stairs.

Jessica felt like a little girl being reprimanded. "I'll be right down." The same knot of anxiety that she'd had in her stomach since… The underarms of her blouse were damp. Why was Mother so upset?

Jessica went downstairs and sat in the floral-patterned armchair in the living room. Her mother went to the kitchen and came back with yet another glass of wine.

"You're not yourself," Mother said. "You seem depressed, honey. If you're in some kind of trouble, legal or otherwise, our attorney friend Sam Elk lives in Portland, and he's trustworthy." She cleared her throat and added, "Also, I've been thinking about the two of us taking a vacation." She paused. "Maybe tour Europe?"

"What?" Jessica swallowed, hard. Her mother seemed to think that everything could be solved with another glass of wine and a referral to an attorney? "I'll think on it." She stood, walked to the kitchen herself and poured herself another large glass of wine.

"Mother," she said, frowning, "I'm going to go rest and think about all this. I am very tired." She gulped the wine and left, glancing at Charles, still in his soft armchair, his face still empty of any expression.

Why had she thought that going home, even for a weekend, would help? She knew so little about her mother, who had spent Jessica's entire life working as a CEO for a multibillion-dollar corporation and was now one of Seattle's foremost millionaires. She thought briefly about visiting her father, who had remarried and now lived in Bellingham, Washington some 90 miles north of Seattle. But that thought soon died. All she ever heard from him was a litany of aches and complaints. He'd spent little time with her when she was a child, and had never expressed any real interest in her life. She spent the rest of the weekend in her childhood bedroom studying her medical journals, determined to do something productive with her time.

When Jessica returned to Portland the next Monday, she drove to the office of Mr. Sam Elk on Burnside Street. Maybe her mother's suggestion was worth checking out. She'd never had the courage to go to the police and report what had happened to her. Right after the rape, she couldn't face even the thought of what she had read were called "rape kits", or imagine answering questions put by possibly skeptical cops. And later, well, they'd just ask her why she hadn't reported the crime when it first happened. So maybe talking with a lawyer would be good.

She walked into an office that was nothing like what she would have thought her mother would approve of. It was bare bones, no clients, not even a receptionist. Mr. Sam Elk was obviously not a man of wealth.

She tapped on a small bell on the corner of the only desk, but no one came. She tapped several times again, and then turned to leave, at which point a door to an office on the left burst open and a brassy voice echoed throughout the waiting area. "How can I help you?" Heavy footsteps were followed by the entrance of the man: about 40, not a single gray wisp in his mop of wild hair, dyed coal black. He had a roll of fat around the middle but was otherwise average with reedy arms. She could see a hint of a tattoo beneath one of his short sleeves.

"Snake," she said softly, staring at his arm.

"Yes, I had that done after Nam." He smiled, but there was sadness in it. *Also, something of a scholarly attitude,* she thought, *like a stockbroker who never saw the sun.* She wondered if he had any tattoos on his shoulder.

"Please, step into my office." He motioned her to a seat, walked behind his desk and sat on a well-worn, black vinyl chair. He leaned back and folded his arms across his belly. The chair creaked ominously. She looked around the room. A wall held bookshelves with legal texts and ring binders, with one large painting of wild horses stampeding through what looked like the Steens Mountain Range. A gooseneck lamp sat on the corner of Mr. Elk's desk. He repeated, "How can I help, Miss…?"

"My name is Sissy Flores," she lied. She didn't want him knowing anything about her. "I have a question."

"Shoot."

"What's the statute of limitations for rape in the state of Oregon?"

He stood, walked to the coffee maker in the corner, and poured himself a cupful.

"Coffee?" he asked.

"No, thanks."

"Is this a minor you're inquiring about?"

"No. This woman is in her 20s."

"Did she recognize her attacker?"

Jessica took a deep breath. "No," she said firmly. "The attack occurred after midnight over a year ago."

The attorney's facial expression changed, and she knew he was aware that she was the victim. He asked, "Do you want me to represent the victim?"

"No, I don't think so," she said. Not this man with his fat belly and drab office.

"Let me tell you something. I handled a case of rape a year ago. The rapist wasn't prosecuted because the statute of limitations had expired by the time he was caught. Three years—that's it. Three years of hiding out and that scumbag got off scot-free. I hope that one day soon the statute will be extended." He closed his eyes, took a long pause and said in an unaffected manner, "Can I be of further help?"

Jessica stood, extended her hand and said, "Thank you for your time. How much do I owe you?"

"Nothing. Let's call this a charitable service."

She turned and rushed to her car.

Arriving back at home, Jessica stepped inside her apartment and slammed the door shut. "Damn." she muttered. She just had to get hold of Leslie's list of party guests. She'd never asked, because then she might have had to tell her friend why she wanted the list. And she'd never told anybody about the rape. Only in that instant did it occur to her that babysitting Leslie's children might create the perfect opportunity to search for such a list. She knew it existed, what with

Leslie's penchant for note taking.

Desperation was settling in. She felt certain the rapist might be a doctor of some sort or someone in the medical field, or maybe a doctor's husband. The tattoo might be enough evidence to convict him and send him to prison for life. The bald eagle symbolized the United States, and it occurred to her, not for the first time, that the rapist might have served in the military. *Enough thinking, at least for tonight.* She took two sleeping pills, got undressed and ran a hot bath, gingerly easing her tense body into the hot water and feeling the tightness soak out of her neck and shoulder muscles. She stretched out in the tub and relaxed, thinking. *Why did the rapist attack me on Leslie's premises? And, could he have known me?*

She felt drowsy; the hot bath and sleeping pills had done their job. She pulled herself out of the tub, dried with a fluffy towel, and put on a nightgown. She set the alarm clock for five. I'll *contact Leslie tomorrow,* she thought. And she fell into a deep, dog-tired sleep.

CHAPTER SIX

Oregon Health and Science University Hospital sat on the crest of a large hill overlooking the downtown area. Jessica had just completed her morning rounds and was momentarily gazing out through the window behind the nurses' station. The view was lost on her. These days, whenever she stopped to rest, thoughts of her attacker crowded in. She had failed to identify him. Time was running out. The statute of limitations was nearing its end. She needed to get that list of partygoers from Leslie.

Fortuitously, the phone rang. One of the nurses said in a loud voice, "Dr. Tinker, this call is for you."

"Thank you." Jessica stepped to the edge of the nurse's station and picked up the phone. "Hello."

"Jessica this is Leslie, I'm so pleased I got hold of you. Can you baby-sit tonight? The nanny is down with the flu, Alexander has to work late on a case, and I have to leave town for the night. If possible, come before five."

My first break, she thought, and said "No problem, but I can't be there until five. Is that okay?"

"Absolutely."

At five minutes past five, a frantic Jessica hurried to her car and sped to Leslie's. She dashed toward the door, and as she lifted her arm about to knock, the door opened.

"You're late," said Leslie, and she bolted out the door.

"I got hung up at the hospital. You know how that happens." Leslie was already at the car, however, and didn't even hear her.

Time passed quickly in games. The grandfather clock rang out the seventh hour, surprising her, and she realized Alexander would be coming home soon. She sprinted into the kitchen and heated up the mac-n-cheese Leslie had left for their dinner, watched the kids as they ate, and then bathed them hurriedly and tucked them into bed.

When she turned on the lights in Leslie's study, she saw a desk, file cabinets and shelves filled with medical books, journals and other neatly arranged paraphernalia. Hurriedly, she looked through the desk drawers and file cabinets. Leslie was organized and compulsive about details, whether medical, social or personal. In a file labeled 'P' she found the party list. With feverish excitement she copied all the data, and then glanced at her watch. "Just past eight," she muttered.

Seconds later, the doorbell rang. She jumped, then stuffed Leslie's list back into the file folder, back into the file cabinet, and her copy of the names into her pocket. She raced for the living room, plunked herself down on the sofa, and waited for Alexander to enter. He didn't. Instead, the doorbell continued to ring.

Jessica opened the door. A man stood on the front doorstep and said, "I'd like to speak with Mr. Snow. My name is Nick Ballard, the next-door neighbor."

Nick Ballard was of average height with a broad chest and a sturdy neck. He looked tough as a rhino. His eyes were like pieces of hot coal. He shifted from one leg to the other with both hands in his trouser pockets. "I need to speak with Alexander now!" His words were sharp and his voice was impatient.

"He'll be home any moment. I'll let him know you called." She shut the door quickly and bolted the lock. Transfixed by fear, she stood rooted to the spot, her heart pulsating and a chilling current passed through her body. *Did this man attend Leslie's parties?* She couldn't recall ever seeing him before, but... *was he the rapist?*

This fear came upon her now every time she encountered a man she hadn't met before. She wanted to find her attacker and beat him senseless or, better yet, eliminate him from planet Earth!

Minutes later, Alexander walked in with a cheerful, "Hi Jessica, how was babysitting? I see you're still alive." He chortled, threw his jacket and briefcase on the sofa, and thanked her for looking after the children.

She forced a smile and said, "Everything went well. A Mr. Ballard came over just a minute ago and asked to speak with you." Quickly picking up her jacket and satchel, she bid him goodnight and left in haste.

When Jessica arrived at her apartment, she immediately fixed herself a cup of Lipton's, took the list from her satchel, sat in her recliner, and worked on compiling a portfolio on everyone she knew who was at that party, along with everyone she didn't know as well.

Before beginning work the next morning, she went to the medical library to work on her academic documentation. Every resident had to maintain complete records of all educational activities performed in surgery. She had a lot of catching up to do, transforming scribbled notes into the required surgical logs, researching techniques and writing papers. She became totally absorbed in her studies, only noticing her surroundings again hours later, having become distracted by lower back discomfort, aching shoulders and the emptiness in her stomach. She stood, stretched, and glanced at her watch—three o'clock.

She collected her books and papers, stuffed everything as neatly as she could into her satchel and dashed downstairs to the first floor. She found a table in the coffee shop and ordered a bagel with cream cheese, a chocolate chip cookie and black coffee. While she ate, she pulled out the list of party goers, ran her finger down the page … and stopped at Max's name.

Oh no! Ice shot through her body. *Could he be the rapist?* He didn't seem overly aggressive or foul-mouthed, but he did have the right build and assertiveness. Her mind raced. The three-year statute of limitation for rape was close to ending. One moment she felt helpless, the next filled with rage, then back to helpless, as though the earth was giving way beneath her and she was falling into an abyss.

Jessica forced herself to read more of the names on the list: Ballard, Gunner, Diesel, Stout, Brown, Bask, Alexander's assistant and several other unfamiliar names, along with a double-digit number of women. For some reason she couldn't fathom, she paused at the name Dr. Dave Bask.

Dr. Bask was a man of few words who obviously loved being a professor. Colleagues described him as quiet, soft-spoken and a loner. He'd recently lost his wife of 30 years to cancer. Before class one day,

Jessica had heard him say to a fellow professor that he always tried to "build confidence in these students without pandering to their egos". No, he didn't seem to fit the profile of the attacker or a rapist.

She went back to the list. Gunner. She couldn't recall seeing Gunner at the party the night of her assault. Her cell phone rang, interrupting her train of thought. For a moment, she decided to ignore it, but then habit set in and she grabbed it out of her satchel. "Hello."

"Jessie, how are you? I haven't called this past week because of my work schedule. I want to take you to the coast this weekend. What do you think?" said Silas.

"Silas! I would enjoy spending the weekend with you."

"Great! I'll pick you up later this afternoon." His voice was high-spirited.

The more she dated him the better she understood him. She thought she might even be falling in love with him, not because he was handsome and smart, but because he was kind.

The weekend brought warm sunny weather with a slight breeze to the coast. They strolled along the beach at a small coastal community and talked about their medical specialties and their future. Silas told her that he had found his niche: working with Dr. Diesel on research projects was as rewarding as a career could get. He turned to face her, eyes sparkling. Then unexpectedly, he picked her up and spun her in a circle, while she erupted in laughter. Time and time again during their conversation, Jessica wanted to confide in this man, to tell him everything. But she simply couldn't bring herself to tell him about the rape.

She knew she had to, though. She had to tell somebody. That evening, with tears flooding her face, she told him everything: the place, date, time, and how it happened. Then she just leaned her head against his chest.

"Oh, Jessie! I'm so sorry such a horrific thing was forced on you. Do the police have any suspects in mind? Do you have any ideas?"

"No." She didn't tell him that she'd not notified the police. "I think it's someone connected with the medical field since this occurred moments after I left the Snow's party."

"Understand, Jessie, I'll support you in any way I can." He kissed her lovingly and said, "Come." They stood and stepped toward the small fridge in the room, and each took out a small bottle of whiskey and poured it over ice.

"Silas raised his whiskey glass, kissed her on the cheek and said, "To many good days ahead!"

CHAPTER SEVEN

O
n an early October Monday morning at 7:00 o'clock, Jessica pushed down on the horizontal slat of a Venetian blind and saw freezing rain bombard the window of the surgical floor at the hospital. Ice covered the fir tree boughs and leafless maple and sweet gum trees, and tree limbs, laden with ice, snapped, resounding like pistol shots. She turned and walked down the narrow hallway toward the doctors' lounge past the framed pictures of former hospital executives and CEOs along the walls. Max was leaning against a windowsill in the doctors' lounge when she came in.

"Good morning, Max."

"Oh, hi." He was frowning.

"Are you all right?" she asked.

"Yes, I'm fine. Just got a lot to think about."

His voice was firm, but he seemed edgy. His eyes were puffy and his posture, as he turned from the window, was more like an old man's than his normal energetic self.

He looks worse than I feel, she said to herself.

"Is there anything I could help with?" she asked.

"No," Max replied. Then, "On second thought, do you have a moment to spare? I'd like to discuss something with you."

"Sure. I have time."

"I just need to share my thoughts with someone who will listen and understand my position. I'm aware you've just entered your second year of residency, but you seem more mature, maybe more worldly, than some of your colleagues. I trust you'll keep what I say confidential." He cleared his throat and continued. "I've been offered a position on the medical board of the hospital and a full-time, seasoned professorship on the faculty. Of course, I'd have to report to Dr. Gunner." She heard him make a small gurgling sound. Then, he said, "This offer wouldn't go into effect for a few months. Do you have an opinion about what I should do?"

Jessica replied, "Well, Max, that depends. I don't know you well enough to make an expert assessment, but I see two options. You could either make a pile of money working long hours to establish your business, or you could agree to work 8-10 hours a day with a reasonable salary, but you'd have to deal with rigid guidelines and rules. And of course, there's the politics." After a brief moment, she blurted, "Then, there's Gunner, whose driving engine is power over everyone. He's someone you'd have to deal with, and that could be intolerable. The important question is, what do you *really* want?"

He crinkled his brow, closed his eyes and said, "I really don't know at this time." Reaching into his jacket, he pulled out a pack of cigarettes, took one out and lit it. "My shift is over. I'm going to head out and get a beer."

"I'm sorry I wasn't much help," Jessica said. She glanced at her watch and said, "I must get to work." She wasn't more than a few steps back into the hallway when she heard a voice cry out, followed by a considerable thud. "Goddamn it! Someone help me!" It was Max, already being assisted by several medical personnel. He had slipped on ice and fallen. "Careful," he winced, "My left leg hurts. I may have fractured it."

Immediately, he was placed on a stretcher and taken into the Emergency Room. Jessica tried to follow, but the door swung closed almost in her face. She did have rounds, so she decided she couldn't just hang around and see what happened.

She didn't hear from Max the rest of the day, and with almost twice as many emergencies as usual in the ER, she had almost forgotten about him. The next morning, he paged her and told her what had happened, asking if she could see him before he was discharged.

"Sure. I'll be in surgery till eleven, and I'll drop by afterward." Jessica wished she'd been able to examine him in the Emergency Room. Doing an exam would've given her the opportunity to see if he had a tattoo of a bald eagle on his shoulder.

Jessica arrived in Max's room shortly before eleven Tuesday morning. "How are you feeling? She asked, her eyes wide, wondering what he wanted. She had little interest in Max on a personal level; she had Silas on her mind. But she admired and respected the knowledge and surgical skills that Max possessed, and thought of him as an open-minded preceptor.

Max apparently needed to talk. He said he'd been preoccupied yesterday and not paying attention to the ice on the steps outside the doctors' lounge. "I used to enjoy the beginning of each week," he said. "Monday was always the best day to discuss new issues with the administration, learn about policy changes, and discuss the resident's complaints. But when I thought of the position I was being offered, I realized I would no longer be perceived as one of the doctors. I myself would be part of the administration, and some of the residents would be complaining about me. I hate to think about it."

"On the other hand," he continued, "establishing a private practice would give me control of my own destiny and eventually bring in more money." He also said he thought it would be nice if, after graduation—and here he looked at her carefully—Jessica could join the business.

"I feel lousy. All I needed was a fracture. Jessica, I called you to let you know I appreciated your earlier opinion and honesty," he ended.

"Think nothing of it. Guess you'll be off your feet for a few days," she said, teasing him and grinning. "But if I can help, let me know. Take care of yourself." She was gone before he could say another word.

Jessica decided to walk to the newly-finished addition of the research lab to see Silas. As she stepped into the lab, Dr. Diesel, the head research analyst, greeted her. "Hello. Silas stepped out for a moment. Perhaps you can come back later."

"Thank you" was all she said. Then, after a pause, "I'm pleased you remembered meeting me in the coffee shop."

Seth Diesel was tall and had a pasty face. She decided he was not remarkable in any way. His eyes were a vague hazel color and his hair a tangle of drab oatmeal color. "Dr. Diesel," she said, glancing about, "How do you like your new lab? It sure looks nice."

His face was more interesting when he smiled. He said, "It's long overdue, and it's nice to have Silas here. Let me give you a quick tour." They stepped around the corner, and she saw beautiful white furry rabbits with pink noses and ears.

"What are these going to be used for?" pointing to the cages nearest her.

"Oh, those will be involved in cancer studies. These rabbits have malignant tumors. But as you know, we will be doing a double blind study, whereby 10 rabbits will receive an experimental drug, and the other 10 will get a placebo. This particular study will take about six months, and by then we hope to know if the drug is effective and if there are any harmful side effects. If everything goes well, in the next phase the drug will be used in human studies."

Jessica thanked Dr. Diesel for the overview and wished him well with the experiments. She left the lab and walked down the hallway, but turned her head to look back when she saw Dr. Gunner entering the lab. She wondered what the two men had in common. Dr. Diesel had no use for any of his colleagues.

Jessica headed for the coffee shop. Before entering, she saw Silas getting two cups of coffee. She watched as he sat down next to a beautiful woman who looked like she might be a Jamaican. She was angry. No, she was jealous. No, anxious. A shudder descended her spine like a wave of electricity. She felt she must be with Silas and tell him she loved him; assert her rights to him, so to speak. But her instinct told her not to. It was too soon. And she didn't know whether….

Jessica turned on her heels and left the coffee shop with a sigh and a pounding heart. She was almost crying. Feeling rejected was painful, but the thought of losing Silas forever was unbearable. She took a deep breath and then decided to drive to the Chart House, a nice restaurant built on a hillside on Terwilliger Street not far from her apartment and relatively close to the hospital. A good meal in a calm environment would settle her.

The parking lot at the Chart House held two cars, and two bicycles were by the front door. Jessica entered the restaurant and seated herself at a table near a window overlooking residential homes and the highway. Three tables away and next to a window sat an unaccompanied, striking man; he was muscular and he gave an impression of power. She was instantly attracted, which really wasn't like her at all. To be smitten with a man she didn't even know. She shook her head.

A waiter arrived, handed her a menu and asked, "Can I get you anything to drink?"

"Yes. A glass of Coors Light please." She was looking the menu over when the man stood up, walked over and said genially, "Hi, my name is Antony Scolari. Do you mind if I join you?"

"If you wish. My name is Jessica Timbers." She wondered if he made a habit of interrupting women and she of lying.

Antony wore tight jeans and a tight white T-shirt. His thigh muscles seemed ready to split the denim, and the veins in his biceps and slightly hairy forearms stood out, with muscles rippling underneath. She was staring. He caught her. She looked away. She wondered what his body would look like after he removed the shirt, the jeans, and even his underwear. It would be like peeling back the layers of an onion.

Jessica cleared her throat, took a consciously casual sip of beer, and turned to the waiter when he asked if they were ready to order.

"I'll have a cup of vegetable soup and bacon-lettuce-and-tomato sandwich," she said.

"And I'll have a medium-rare sirloin steak and a glass of Coors."

Antony said. Then, turning to Jessica, he said, "Well, Jessica do you live around here?"

"Actually I do. How about you? Do you live and work here?"

With his hands folded and resting on the table, Antony looked at her, smiled and said, "Yes. Matter of fact, I'm working on a project not too far from here. I was contracted to build a new extension to the hospital research center and renovate the War Veterans' Building. We've been on the project for a couple of months."

Jessica knew the building he was talking about. The veterans' hospital was a three-story building with three wings extending outward like huge claws sprawled along the hillside.

"Sounds like a big undertaking. Are you in construction or management?"

"I supervise all aspects of design and construction, but professionally, I'm an architect."

Jessica finished her meal, glanced at her watch, and then said, "I've got to go. A lot of things to do."

"I'd like to see you again. Take you to a movie. Is that possible?" She was trying to decide whether she wanted to get to know this hunk of a man when he added, "I'll pick you up at your home. How about this Friday?" His gaze rested on the pale saddle of freckles over the bridge of her nose. He seemed to assume she was available.

She felt tingling, and her stomach fluttered. Her mouth watered just as it did when she saw lemon meringue pie. "I'll meet you here. It's more convenient for me. How about six-thirty?"

"Fine."

"She stood, said good bye and left, leaving him with the bill.

CHAPTER EIGHT

When Friday evening arrived, Jessica still hadn't heard from Silas. She was tempted to contact him, but not knowing whether he'd be at the lab or with that beautiful woman stopped her. *Why had he not at least called? Well, maybe something happened.*

She walked into the living room and glanced at his photo placed strategically in the center of the living room oak table next to a lamp. His eyes sparkled, even in a photograph. Alone, she admitted she felt rejected by him even though she had to recognize that it was unreasonable. *After all,* she said to herself, *he was from Jamaica. The woman could be a colleague from that country, or a cousin, or even just a friend.* "Well, whatever," she said to herself. She had a date with Antony at six-thirty after work.

The clock chimed 7:00 in the morning. Jessica parted the curtains and saw gusts of wind swaying the Douglas fir trees and dense clouds sweeping across a dreary sky. For a few minutes, she wondered why she was so smitten by Antony. Maybe she'd solve that mystery tonight. She collected her good sense, along with the papers and books she'd use for the day, packed her satchel and had a quick breakfast of toast with peanut butter and instant coffee.

She felt more invigorated as she drove to work and then better yet, as she stepped out of her car and took a few deep, cold breaths. She entered the surgical floor with the usual spring in her step even though she realized she was a few minutes late.

Dr. Stout greeted her. "Hello Jessica. What's new?" He always made her feel calm and competent.

"Nothing special. Actually nothing," she paused. Then, barely audible, she whispered, "Sorry I'm late."

He didn't seem concerned about her tardiness. "When nothing's new, it means things must be all right," he said cheerfully. "We need to see a case in the Emergency Room."

She wondered if she'd been destined to see a double-digit number of patients in the ER with this particular doctor. However, she was pleased since he was so kind, and a great teacher, too.

When the two of them entered the ER, one of the nurses told them the patient was in the fourth cubicle. Jessica pulled back the curtain to find a girl, no more than perhaps 16, with blood dripping out of her left ear. The girl was still, staring sightlessly at the ceiling, her face ashen. Jessica placed her stethoscope on the girl's chest, hoping to hear heartbeats or respiration. Nothing. Dead. Her chart held a police report that said she'd been strangled and raped and had sustained a blow to the head.

Jessica stood over the youngster's body. She raised her gaze to Dr. Stout. Her fear must be obvious. "She's gone," she said in a whisper, her eyes filling with tears.

He nodded.

Two policemen stood outside the emergency room. They introduced themselves and asked Jessica if she had any medical information that could aid in their investigation. "No, not at this time," she said, and walked to the doctors lounge. She sat on a small sofa there, feeling frozen. It was shock, she knew. The sight of the girl's open, staring, eyes…

She is afraid. She has been afraid ever since. She's sitting on a sofa now, but she can still feel the cold ground. She sees people at tables in front of her, sipping coffee, but she always seems to be gazing sightlessly at a sky above. She's still waiting for him to come back.

"This could've been me." Her elbows are on her knees. Her hands are supporting her head.

Just then, Dr. Stout stepped into the lounge. "Are you all right?" he asked.

"I'm fine." She swallowed, hard, and gave voice to her anger. "I hope the police capture and kill the lowlife who committed this murder." She wished Silas were here to share her anger and sadness.

"This truly is a tragedy," said Dr. Stout. He had moved back a step, seemingly taken aback by her response.

At five-forty, Jessica's shift ended, leaving her enough time to comb her hair, apply lipstick, get her jacket and drive to the Chart House Restaurant to meet Antony. Once inside, she immediately spotted him and headed for his table. He stood, slid a chair back for her to sit down and seated himself across from her. He wore a Harris-tweed jacket, trousers, and a pullover sweater of a dark green color, like the foliage on a pine tree. His color choice accentuated his olive complexion, brown eyes and ebony hair. Yes, she did feel powerfully attracted to him.

"Well, Jessica, how have you been?" he asked with a broad smile.

"Fine." That was a lie. She tried to erase the images of the teenager in the ER and of her own attack. "What movie will we be seeing?" she asked.

"*One Flew Over the Cuckoo's Nest*. It's about a brash rebel who rallies the patients to take on the oppressive Nurse Ratchet, a woman more a dictator than a nurse."

"Wow! Sounds exciting." *My God, I don't need to see or hear anything about medicine, hospitals and death*, she thought.

There was a large crowd in the movie theater for the showing. They sat in the back row of the theater. Jessica couldn't think of anything to say, and the silence stretched out until he asked if she'd like some popcorn. Her flat "No, thank you" seemed impersonal even to her.

She hadn't wanted anything at all after dinner, but when he returned with the popcorn, she snatched the bag from him and scarfed down more than half of it, only then handing it back to him. *Nervous,* she told herself. *Even more so after what I've seen today.*

During the movie, Antony took her hand. Their fingers intertwined, sending tingles through her body. The movie lasted too long, the popcorn not long enough.

When the credits rolled, Antony asked, "Would you like to come to my apartment? Maybe you'd like to see the architectural design models for the renovation of the veterans' hospital and the expansion to the research lab?" He was appealing to her insightful and intellectual nature, and that seemed safe. So she said, "Okay. But I can only stay for a short time."

"Fair enough. Your car or mine?"

"I'll follow you."

Antony had a small apartment in a recently constructed building downtown. They got off the elevator on the 8th floor, he unlocked a door, and they stepped inside. A modest living room was neat and clean with a sofa, two chairs, a desk and a chipped ceramic lamp. A kitchen table held a large book, and architectural sheets of paper hung over the chair. She wondered where the models were.

He stepped toward her and said, "Let me help you with your jacket. Could I offer you a glass of wine?"

"Please." She felt suddenly as though she were in a cage. She followed him into the kitchen.

"Is chardonnay okay? His smile got her heart rate up several notches, and to cover up her reaction she flashed him a bright smile and said, "Yes."

He waited a moment as if unsure how to proceed then said, "Let me show you the designs." He picked up the design sheets and spread them across the table. She stepped closer to see as his finger traced the layout of the new research addition. He gently placed his arm around her waist, then, and continued explaining the design.

Jessica felt she was spinning out of control. She drifted toward Antony, drawn by the evident pride in his voice as he spoke about his design, and equally by her own desire and raging emotions. Then Antony's arms encircled her. He turned her to face him and rained kisses on her eyelids, down her cheeks and ears. He whispered, "You must know as well as I what's happening," and his lips found hers. She succumbed to yearning and returned his kisses.

"Jessica," he moaned, "you're beautiful. Achingly beautiful." His words seemed to wrap themselves around her, alluring, charming, wanting. He whisked her off her feet and into his arms and carried her into the darkness of his bedroom. Her head was crushed against his chest and she heard the pounding of his heart. He was a mad stranger in the darkness, carrying her with strong arms. She made a small woofing sound, muffled against him. Laying her on his bed, he bent over her and then, with savagery and totality, wiped out everything from her mind except excitement, joy, fear, and madness. Her arms were around his neck, his legs between hers. They floated into anonymity.

Before sunrise, Jessica opened her eyes and found herself wrapped around Antony's legs. He seemed to be in a deep sleep. Slowly, she maneuvered out of bed, gathered her clothes strewn on the floor and tiptoed into the bathroom.

Staring at herself in the mirror made her feel sick; sick with guilt and shame at what she'd done. She thought the madness had taken hold of her. Splashing cold water on her face didn't alter anything. She dressed without showering, finger combed her hair, applied lipstick and quietly opened the bathroom door—and there stood Antony, looking like a large unmade bed and demanding, "Where are you going?"

"Home." Fear nudged at her.

"Stay for a cup of coffee. And let's talk. I have something to tell you," he intoned.

"There's nothing to say. I must go." She wanted to tell him how stupid she'd been.

"Jessica, why the rush?"

She grabbed her satchel and jacket and said, "Goodbye, Antony." She fled.

CHAPTER NINE

Late Monday night, Jessica was just getting to asleep when the phone rang. On the fourth ring, she managed to wake up enough to answer it. "Yes?"

"Hello," It was Silas. "How are you? I want to…"

Jessica interrupted, "What do you want? It's very late. I've got a lot to do tomorrow."

"Jessie, please listen," he said, as if he read her mind about being upset. "A friend of mine from Jamaica, Fawn Juzel, isn't well. She's trying to find someone to care for her son while she's receiving chemotherapy for malignant tumors in her abdomen and kidney. She doesn't have much time left."

"It's nice of you to lend a hand," she replied, her voice succinct and distant.

"Jessie, I'd rather not discuss this at length on the phone. Can we meet at seven o'clock for breakfast at the hospital café?"

"Fine. I'll see you there. Bye."

She felt… what? Pleasure at the thought of seeing Silas again, but it was mixed with intense guilt about her night with Antony, and for wanting to hurt Silas for not calling. Feeling rejected was painful.

When she entered the coffee shop the next morning, Silas was seated in a booth drinking coffee and looking at the menu. When she approached the booth, he stood, put his arms around her, gave her a kiss on the cheek and said, "Good morning. I hope you're hungry."

The waiter approached the table and Silas ordered a mushroom omelet, toast and coffee. Jessica ordered black coffee and one slice of toast.

"Is that all you're having?" he asked.

"Yes, I'm feeling tired and not hungry this morning."

"Jessie, would you like to go to the coast this weekend?" He cleared his throat, and there were those sparkling eyes looking at her once more. "I'd like to see the coast again."

Despite her confusion, she smiled. She was in love —madly in love.

"Before I forget, Jessie, I'll be attending a conference on cancer research in Maui for two weeks."

"That sounds educational. When do you leave?"

"Thursday of next week. That's why I want to get away with you on the weekend, so we'll have time together before I leave. Jessie, I hope you understand why I didn't call this last week. As I mentioned before, Fawn is very ill and needs a lot of attention."

Jessica was about to say something that would indicate she had completely forgiven him for not calling, but just then Seth walked into the coffee shop and slid into the booth next to Silas.

"Good morning. I'm starved. By the way, the conference at Maui will address the latest cancer research findings. No doubt you'll learn a great deal."

After breakfast, Silas gave Jessica a hug and a kiss, and then each went their own way. Halfway to the surgical ward, Jessica's stomach rumbled. She was still hungry, so she went back to the restaurant and ordered a takeout cappuccino and a cinnamon roll. She was sitting there waiting for her order when a waiter she hadn't seen before, tall and lean, in his early 20s, asked her what she'd like to order. He looked like a model for a men's magazine. "I'm waiting for my cappuccino to go," she said. Then, looking up, she noticed Antony approaching her table. He was wearing his tight jeans with a V-neck sky blue cotton sweater. She would have rather seen most anyone other than him.

"Hello, Jessica. I saw you racing down the hallway earlier. What are you doing here? Are you a nurse here or something?"

"Oh no," she mumbled. She knew now that Antony thought of himself as prince charming, and right now he was last person she wanted to see. She felt so much regret. Had she permitted herself to be used? Was her love life neurotic? She choked back a sob.

"Jessica." He sat down across the table, took a breath, and launched into what she thought might be a rehearsed speech. "I need to tell you…" He stopped, eyes darting from her to the window and then back at her. "I can't ever see you again. You see…" he faltered, arms on the table and hands clasped. "I'm married. My wife and I have a 3 year old."

She looked at him – utterly empty of feeling, like a toy, unable to move her body.

"That's all I have to say. I'm sorry." He stood, turned and left.

Jessica sat a few more minutes until the waiter announced that her cappuccino and roll were ready. She stood, her body trembling, picked up her drink and took a long sip. Rage engulfed her like an incoming tide. She wasn't some hooker to be picked up at a coffee shop and taken to his apartment to spend the night. *With how many other women, some of them other men's wives, had he been cheating on his wife?*

She practically stumbled back down the hall toward the surgical ward—and there were Dr. Gunner and Antony together. Both were laughing and behaving like long-lost buddies. Dr. Gunner was even patting Antony on the back. She turned quickly before they could see her, dashed around a corner and entered an elevator. Her heart was beating too fast. This was all too much.

What was the connection between these two men? I must find out!

It was a dark that evening. Rain fell in big drops. There would be a storm before morning. Jessica was on the verge of despair after the incident with Antony and a long busy day at the hospital. The first thing she did when she arrived home was to head for the vodka and then her recliner. After her drink, she felt woozy and went straight to bed. How nice it would be have Silas by her side...

∗ ∗ ∗

By late November, Jessica was experiencing nausea. She had even vomited several times, once at work. She had no appetite and had lost five pounds in two months. She knew stress could precipitate such symptoms, but she'd also missed two periods. And her periods had always been very regular, almost always beginning on the same day each month. She had to be sure.

The next morning, she drove to a drugstore several miles away from her apartment. She found a pregnancy test kit and, not being able to spot anyone she knew, quickly paid cash for the kit and went directly home. Several glasses of water made it possible to obtain a urine sample.

She tested it, and the results were positive. She was pregnant.

She felt hollow, as though she weren't even alive. She wished she could just will herself dead. A tear tracked down her cheek.

After a while, she got up and called the hospital, informed the secretary to relay her message to the senior surgery resident that she wouldn't be reporting for work because of illness. Of course, that was a lie. So now she was lying on top of being a slut—and getting pregnant. Suddenly she panicked. How would Silas react? He'd never believe he fathered this baby since, without fail, he'd used a condom.

For the rest of the day, she tried to figure out what to do. She could defer her studies, take some base-pay job where nobody knew her, have the baby and be a single parent—and live on base pay with a kid for years with nobody to ask for help even if she got sick.

OK, then, since I'm only two months pregnant, I could have an abortion. She thought about this long and hard before she rejected it. It was against the spiritual values of life. *What about having the baby and giving it up for adoption?* Then she remembered her mother's offer to travel to Europe. That seemed the easiest course of action.

Later that afternoon, Jessica looked out her living room window. Dark clouds hung in the air. Rain would come soon. A crash of distant thunder seemed to echo her inner turmoil. She stood motionless for a prolonged period of time, and then decided to take a cool shower.

Standing under the water, she messaged her tummy and found herself talking to her unborn baby. "What am I supposed to do? I can't raise you alone—school, work, and studies. I don't think I can go through an abortion. The best thing for you would be to give you up for adoption." She lifted her face, and her tears mixed with the droplets of water. "Give you away like a discarded coat," she moaned. This would be so heartless.

She stepped out of the shower, dressed and crawled into her recliner. She wanted a drink, but that wouldn't be good for the baby. *Maybe just a sip of wine?* No, not even that would be good.

Just then the phone rang. Before she could say more than a hello, Silas said, "Jessie, I'm calling to let you know that Seth and I will be leaving in the morning for Eugene for that two-day conference." There was a slight pause, and then he said, "I will need to visit Fawn before I go. I'll call you as soon as I return. I love you, Jessie."

Jessica decided to just ignore information he imparted to her about this Fawn person. After all, Silas would be allowed to have friends, and she would have her friends, too. She replied, "I love you, too, and I'll miss you. Silas, are you sure you can't come over tonight?"

"I'll call you when I return, Jessie."

Suddenly, her head felt congested, her hearing became muffled. She shook her head like a dog would shake to remove water from its coat, realizing again that Silas almost certainly would not accept the baby.

March had arrived, and Jessica was in her fifth month, when she finally decided to tour Europe. She had been successful at hiding her pregnancy, but her studies and her performance at work were both suffering. She made out an itinerary of places she wanted to visit and emailed it to her mother. Her mother replied almost immediately, not with an email but with an excited phone call.

"Mother, sometimes I feel as though I hardly know you, so I'm looking forward to this trip and to spending time with you, getting to know you. I feel…" She paused for a long moment, and then blurted, "I don't want to have the baby in Oregon."

"What? What did you say?" Her mother's voice was suddenly hoarse.

"Mother, I'm pregnant. I'm not sure whether to keep the baby or give it up for adoption."

There was silence on the line. Then, her mother cleared her throat and said, "Maybe you can have the baby in Seattle and stay here with us. What does Silas think?

"Silas doesn't know, and he's not the father."

"Who is?" Her mother sounded choked-up. She coughed.

"It doesn't matter, Mother. Do you think we could leave in a week? I'm five months pregnant, almost six, but I don't look it." It was a rush of words. She was trembling, and the nausea that had gone away in her third month was suddenly back.

"We can leave next week, Jessica."

"Good. I'll see you in a few days." She no sooner hung up when the doorbell rang. She opened the door, and there stood Silas.

"It's so good to see you. How are you?" she asked with some coolness.

"So, I haven't heard from you for some time," he said, sounding peeved. "I've called and left messages. Are you avoiding me?"

"No! Heavens, no. I've been busy… reading, mostly spending time in the library. And planning my trip to Europe. Remember, I mentioned earlier that Mother and I were going to take a trip. Well, you've been so busy that probably didn't even register." She invited him in and motioned to the sofa.

"No, I don't remember," he said, taking a seat. "Where in Europe? How long will you be gone? What about your residency?"

"Mother and I will travel to England and Scotland. We'll be gone for a month or so, maybe less, maybe more. I'll resume my residency when I return."

He stared at her. "You're so beautiful. Why are you leaving for Europe now?" His smile revealed his white teeth against his dark complexion and made her ache. She wanted desperately to tell him about the pregnancy. But how could she? If he knew the baby wasn't his, he would be gone immediately.

"Mother wants me to accompany her to Europe. She hasn't told me why, just that she wants me along. And that's enough for me. I hardly know her, so the trip is an opportunity." True, what she was saying, just not the whole truth. "But we'll keep in touch."

"Come sit by me," he padded the sofa, his mood suddenly seemed happier.

She sat uncertainly beside him and said, "I hope our future holds good things for us."

"It will," he said with confidence. He slid over very close to her, and his lips began an intense exploration of hers.

She just could not respond to him. "Please forgive me," she said, sighing, "but I feel very fatigued, achy, and actually even nauseous."

For a moment he seemed quite disappointed. "Jessie, you do look tired. Actually, you look as though you're about to collapse with stress. And you seem sad. On second thought, I agree you need rest. You know that I love you, and Jessie, let me know if I can be of any help."

"When I return," she said, "I'll finish my surgical residency with renewed energy." She gathered herself for a moment and then added, "Silas, our passion for each other sometimes seems all consuming. I love it. When I return, our love for each other will become even stronger."

"I hope so," Silas replied with a smile.

"I'll call you when we arrive in Europe."

CHAPTER TEN

A mild spring had begun, and native dogwoods and maple trees were beginning to bud. The sky was robin's egg blue with only a few wisps of clouds in the distance. Jessica drove to Seattle feeling more upbeat than she had in a long time. She thought the forthcoming trip to Europe would provide the perfect opportunity to better understand her mother and to review the responsibilities of motherhood. It might even be that coming back to Silas with the baby, along with being an excellent mother and continuing her residency, would influence him positively. She prayed he'd accept her baby. She wanted to make a future with him.

Europe was a whirlwind of sightseeing: from northern Scotland on the Isle of Skye—so quiet and peaceful; to Edinburg, the capital, where they bought woolens her mother would have made into coats back home; to the idyllic beauty of Lake District in England; and finally to the most international of cities—London—which appealed to Jessica the most. It was a place in which she might even consider working, if she could ever finish her residency.

By late March, it was time to return to Seattle. Jessica was now at the end of her sixth month of pregnancy. When she went out now, she wrapped a shawl on her round body. She and her mother laughed at some of the side effects: her feet splayed out and taking up maximum space in her shoes, her fingers puffy. By then, the two of them had made the decision that she would stay in Seattle until the baby was born. Then, announced Jessica, "I'll look for a reputable child-care center in Portland and return to finish my surgical residency."

Her mother couldn't have had a better response: "Honey, I'm looking forward to having a grandchild. I'm pleased you've decided to keep the baby."

Jessica reached over and touched her mother's shoulder. "Me, too" she said.

Her mother smiled, took her hand, and said, "Don't worry about money. We'll be more than pleased to help you." Then, "And it's good that you'll finish school."

"I appreciate your help until I get myself through school." Jessica felt as though a huge load were off her shoulders. She reached over, past her roundness, and hugged her mother. "I'm sorry," she mumbled. "It was dumb and irresponsible of me to get myself pregnant. What I mean is… after what happened to me before… being violated. I don't know what came over me."

"I understand. But honey, everything will turn out well. You'll see. It's probably what God wants for you."

"What God wants…" she repeated. She dragged her sleeve across her eyes and sniffled. Who would know what God would want? All she wanted now was the opportunity to have everything taken care of while she had this baby, and this is what her mother was offering. She was grateful.

Jessica's last telephone contact with Silas had occurred mid-March. She'd told him that her mother wanted to stay in Europe for an indefinite time, so he would not expect her back soon and would have no idea that she was actually in Seattle. Nevertheless, she would eventually have to face him with the news of this new person, and only after that would she find out whether they would have a life together.

The days slipped by, and her body became even larger and more unwieldy, as she attempted to relax in her mother's home in Seattle. Everything made her anxious, and being away from Silas and having her studies interrupted were increasingly frustrating. Her mother noticed.

"Jessica, honey, maybe you need to take up yoga. You seem so wound-up."

"Mother, I don't need yoga or anything else." Not only was that a lie, but it didn't even stop her mother from nagging at her to relax. *As though nagging would help me relax.* She took daily walks, read novels and manicured her fingernails and toenails to perfection—although it seemed that within days she couldn't bend over and do toenail polish touchups.

One day in May, she had intermittent abdominal cramps. She'd calculated her due date to be in late June. She prayed to carry this baby to full term. But as the minutes stretched to hours, irregular contractions evolved into a regular pattern. Finally, between gasps, she shouted, "Mother, I'm in labor. Call an ambulance and take me to the hospital."

As hospital personnel wheeled her onto the maternity floor, her water broke and she continued in labor. It was well after midnight, somewhere near 2:30 in the morning, when in her now-drugged fog of pain and confusion she heard a high-pitched cry. It sounded like the repetitious piece from an opera she and her mother had seen in England. It echoed through the nursery hallway.

The late night hours were cool and still, illuminating thousands of stars visible through her hospital window. *So,* she realized, *I'm back in bed. What happened in the delivery room? I must have passed out.* Then she passed out again, this time awakening to see daylight through the window. She turned her head when she heard the wailing sound again and saw a red-haired nurse carrying something blue into her room. Something screaming and wrapped in blue.

"Here is your 5-pound 10-ounce beautiful baby," the nurse said with a big smile.

Jessica unwrapped the bundle and saw that she had given birth to a boy. She then immediately examined her son's hips, legs and feet. All there and in the right places. She checked his fingers, 10 of them, and felt the soft membrane-covered space between the bones in the baby's skull. Satisfied there were no abnormalities, she put him to breast. He suckled hungrily with a direct practiced air while she stared at his new arrival in her life. Soft wisps of hair looked as though they were woven of solid gold. She wondered if Antony had blond hair as a baby. She gazed into his brown eyes, fixed. They were reflective and open like windows into his soul. He was a beautiful baby. His skin like his father's, his features attractive like his mother's.

The nurse took the baby after he finished nursing and was dozing on her breast. Then, a birth certificate form was handed to Jessica, which she needed to fill out and sign. There were difficulties.

The first one was what to put down on the line that read '*Father's Name*'. She thought about writing Silas's name, but quickly discarded that notion. He should at least know about the baby and decide to take responsibility for him before he was named, falsely, as the father. She certainly was not about to put down Antony's name. Better that man never even know he had a son. She knew that one day her son would need his birth certificate, so this was important. Finally, she put down '*unknown*'.

Then, what to put down for his name? She'd been struggling with this for some time and had narrowed the list down to four names. She'd considered naming him Silas, but certainly not until, and unless, Silas accepted him. She's considered Antony. Antony Jr. would be accurate, but… Then there was *Finnegan*. When she was growing up, her mother had had a friend named Finnegan, and she'd always liked the name. Lastly, *Benjamin* was an obvious choice since that was her grandfather's middle name. Finally, she wrote '*Finnegan Benjamin*'. "But I'll always call him Finny," she said to herself with a smile.

Jessica brought Finny to her mother's home on a chilly but sunny day in May. Her days after that were filled with feeding, burping, changing diapers, rocking, and loving. She believed her baby would always fill her heart with so much love that she wouldn't even care about fathers.

On a warm day in late June, when Finny was five weeks old, Jessica left him in the care of her mother and drove to Portland. It took several days to reacquaint herself with her apartment. She realized she needed to find a larger living space, perhaps a condo. First step, though, was to find day care for her baby. After that, she needed to sit down with Silas and tell him the truth. The whole truth, about how she had gotten pregnant, about being with her mother in Europe and then in Seattle during her pregnancy, and about the baby. She was very much afraid that Silas would be bitter and jealous. If he lost trust in her, she didn't know what she would do.

After several days of waking up in the morning ready to have a conversation with Silas and going to bed at night without having done so, the phone rang. Of course it was Silas.

"Hello?"

"Hello, Jessie!" he said, his voice as always deep and resonant. "Silas here. How are you?"

"Fine. Good morning, Silas."

Briskly, he said, "Jessie, I've been very busy with research and helping Fawn with her child and other chores. Her health is failing very quickly. How was your trip to Europe? You certainly didn't call me much. I called Seattle and talked with your mother. She said you were back here in Portland." Silas' speech was rapid, and he sounded annoyed.

"Silas, the trip was fine. But now, I'm busy with school and finding a larger apartment."

"Why do that?" he asked, sounding judgmental.

"Well…"She struggled for words, and then finally said, "Just because I need more room." After a long pause she said, "Silas, would you have coffee with me this morning?"

"Fine. See you at the Chart House at ten o'clock."

When she arrived at the restaurant, Silas was seated and drinking a cup of coffee. She approached his table and he stood when she stepped by his side. "You look lovely, Jessie. Your ponytail hangs like a flag all the way to your shoulders." They both laughed, but she faked hers.

"I haven't found time to get a hair trim—busy with school and all."

"How have you been?" He looked into her eyes and gave her a long hug and quick kiss.

Looking around, she noticed only a half-dozen customers, all busy talking. *Good. It would be nice not to be overheard.* She sat down, mustered courage, reminding herself that Silas deserved to know about Finny. But a waitress appeared then, so first they had to go through the bother of ordering: a ham sandwich and coffee for Silas; a coffee and scone for her, though what she really wanted was beer, or even vodka.

"Jessie, I'm very happy doing cancer research." He looked at her and smiled. "We can spend more time together now that you're back and will soon go into your third year of residency."

She stretched her hands across the table, grasped his hand and slowly rubbed his fingers.

"Jessie, is everything all right? You seem different . . . nervous."

"Silas, I... I... have something to tell you." Her eyes filled with tears as she repeated, "I have something to tell you."

"Jessie, what is it?"

"It's time... it's time I told you the truth."

"Truth about what?" he asked, sympathetic but perplexed.

"You'll hate me. You can't hate me more than I hate myself for what happened. You'll never marry me. You'll refuse to believe it was unintentional." She was hysterical. "I have a..." She wiped her eyes with the back of her hand, and then pulled a hankie from her pocket. Tears rolled down her cheeks. She gasped for air.

"I have a baby. My mother is looking after him now."

Silas drew back, shocked. "What? What are you talking about?"

"I had an affair and carelessly got pregnant. It was just a fling. It meant nothing, absolutely nothing. I love *you*, Silas."

"A fling?! Jesus Christ, Jessie." He waved a hand in the air, as though to ward off something evil. She could see disgust, then anger, then pain in his expression. "Is that why you went to Europe?"

"Yes. I couldn't bring myself to tell you. I feared you'd leave me. You probably will."

"Whose baby is it? It's not mine. We've always taken precautions. So whose?" He fired questions as if on a battlefield. He dragged his hand through his hair in frustration, his dark eyes wide and disbelieving. "You had an affair with another man, while telling me you're in love with me? Is this the way you're going to share information with me? Make up lies? You call that love? Trust?" His voice went up decibels.

"It doesn't matter whose. Please forgive me," she implored him. By now, the half-a-dozen customers had turned to look at them.

"It's unforgivable. And there I was, all those days and weeks and months, worrying about you, wondering whether you were OK. While you…" Silas got up then, paid the bill and left.

CHAPTER ELEVEN

For four months after Silas stormed out of the Chart House, Jessica didn't hear from him. She remained in her apartment, concentrated on her residency, and tried not to think about him—while thinking about him almost continually. Her baby remained in Seattle, with his grandmother.

By December, she was beginning to recover from the emotional limbo. She still hoped that eventually Silas would forgive her, and that they could resume their relationship. Now, however, she realized it was time to search vigorously for a childcare center for Finny, bring him to Portland, and get on with her life. She put her search into overdrive, checking, observing and interviewing daycare centers all over the city. Weeks later, she walked into a century-old monastery built on a hill with a sweeping vista of the Willamette River, city and skyline. An iron fence around the periphery of the property gave the impression of a gated community. The church stood high above the other buildings, with two tiers of roof at one end.

Inside the church, she knelt and asked God for forgiveness for conceiving Finny in a sinful way. Then, she thought about her rape. "God, how could I ever forgive the bastard who raped me?" she asked Him. She thought if he were here now, she would try to hurt him. She still wanted revenge, even though the statute of limitations had expired. And she did not only feel revenge. She was also afraid for other women he might hurt, might already have hurt.

Then, inhaling deeply and deliberately relaxing her shoulders, she refocused on finding a daycare center. This monastery had residences for children awaiting adoption and for children of working parents. Maybe Finny would get good care here. Seeing a nun genuflect at the altar and then head toward a side door, she quickly stood and approached her. "Sister, could I speak with you for a moment?"

The Sister stopped, turned and said, "Yes, how can I help you?"

"My name is Jessica Tinker" she spoke rapidly. "I'm interested in this daycare center for my child. I'd like some information about the center."

"For adoption or otherwise?" the Sister asked.

"Um, otherwise."

"Very well, follow me to my office. My name is Sister Beatrice. We are the Order of Holy Sanctuary Monastery."

Sister Beatrice was elderly, tall and stout with a notable amount of hair on her upper lip. Her voice was deep, but she seemed gentle. Jessica sat in a wooden chair across the desk from her high-backed chair.

"My dear, how old is your child, and what do you and your husband do?"

"My husband died a few months ago," she paused, feeling heat rise to her cheeks. She lowered her head, feeling the crushing effect of her lie. "I live alone with my son."

"I'm sorry to hear that. How do you support yourself and your son?" Sister Beatrice asked.

"I'm a resident of surgery at the medical school here. My parents live in Seattle and financially support me, I mean us." She hesitated, and then said, "Only until I complete my schooling."

"I see." Sister Beatrice shuffled through a stack of folders on her desk and handed Jessica an application form. "Do fill out the requested number of references." She paused and then added, "Be sure to fill in every line. I will review your application and then schedule an appointment for you to meet with Mother Superior and our admitting committee."

After meeting with Sister Beatrice, Jessica felt more secure about Finny's care. The monastery seemed like a place to find comfort. What would happen, she wondered, if she built her life the way the nuns do… that is, to set aside time throughout the day to pray and ask forgiveness for sinfully conceiving Finny?

While driving to the hospital the next day, she couldn't help smiling, thinking about Finny and his cuddliness, giggles and coos. Her arms ached, wanting to hold him. By the time she reached the hospital, she was missing her baby boy tremendously.

By late afternoon, Jessica placed two ads on the school bulletin board; one for a female roommate who would provide evening care for Finny, and the other for a three-bedroom apartment.

Unbelievable! Within one day she'd leased an apartment, and three days later a young second-year medical student called expressing an interest in being a roommate. An interview was set up at Jessica's apartment at five o'clock the following day.

Cheyenne Clay, when she arrived the next day, proved to be from Cheyenne, Wyoming. "You're looking for a roommate and a sitter?" she asked, her voice exuberant. Jessica asked her in and found out that she had younger brothers whom she had cared for from an early age, her mother being away working, and that she liked children. Jessica promised to check her references and, if they were good, to move her into the third bedroom in her apartment.

A month passed. Jessica was spreading butter on toast one morning when the phone rang. It was Sister Beatrice. She said that the committee was prepared to discuss Jessica's childcare request and that the appointment was scheduled for the following Tuesday at eight o'clock in the morning. Jessica was proud that she had taken care to find people who would help her raise Finny with love and care.

That Monday, Jessica attended a lecture by Dr. Stan Wick, a well-known research oncologist from Dana Farber institute in Boston. Dr. Wick discussed types of cancer, clinical trials, diagnosis, treatment, and finally patient emotions. At the first break, while getting a cup of coffee at the snack table, she felt a tap on her shoulder. Turning, she said, "Max, it's good to see you here."

"Where else would I be?" He grinned mischievously, showing his slightly irregular white teeth. "Wow, you addressed me by my first name in public. How sweet!"

Jessica scanned the room, smiled, and said, "There are a large number of people in attendance."

"A large attendance is a good indicator that people are interested in forefront research in cancer treatment," Dr. Stout replied from across the snack table.

At that moment, the emcee announced that the session was about to resume. "See you gentlemen later," Jessica said and walked back to her chair. She found Max's grin appealing, but at times the man puzzled her. He was controlled and firm one moment, relaxed and witty the next. It made her feel guarded.

After the presentation, she bumped into Max again. He was engaged in what looked like a serious discussion with Drs. Stout and Diesel. All three turned toward her and smiled. "Hi! Are you three enjoying the conference?" she asked, wondering why Silas hadn't attended.

"Absolutely. Great information. The speaker, Stan Wick, is an old friend of mine. We go way back," said Dr. Stout. "Jessica, what did you learn today?"

"Just getting updated on drug research."

Dr. Stout stretched his neck a few inches, glancing over the people in front of him, and said, "Here comes Stan."

Dr. Stout made the introductions before continuing, and then added, "Stan, this hospital just finished adding an extension to the research center. Hopefully, we will be able to do more preclinical studies."

"Damn right, and find qualified research analysts," Dr. Diesel added.

Jessica had the urge to say, "More like Silas—really devoted to the work," but Dr. Diesel's abrasive manner dictated that she keep her mouth shut. Instead, she said, "Excuse me. It's been a pleasure to meet you, Dr. Wick. I enjoyed your presentation. Now, I must go and attend to my duties." As she moved away from them, she could tell that Max was watching her, perhaps even ogling her. It made her feel like a woman.

At eight o'clock Tuesday morning, Jessica stood by the monastery door, inhaled deeply and knocked. She was dressed in a black suit, white V-neck blouse, and two-inch black leather pumps with a matching leather handbag. She knew she looked professional. She was asked to wait in a room that held a table, eight chairs and a bouquet of assorted flowers.

Twenty-five minutes later, she began pacing back and forth. She looked down the hall but saw no one. Finally, at eight-thirty, someone with so much authority that she must be the Mother Superior entered with five nuns in tow, all dressed in black-and-white habits. She thought they resembled penguins marching in line. Jessica stood. The Mother Superior sat in the chair at the head of the table and gestured for the others to be seated. She spoke first.

"Your name is Dr. Jessica Tinker, and you're here about placing your son into our daycare center." A crucifix hung around her neck, which Jessica could not fail to notice, and another was on the wall in front of her. They were intimidating reminders of her sin.

"Let us bow our heads in prayer," said the Mother Superior. She recited the Lord's Prayer and then looked up again at Jessica. "Please tell us why we should accept your child here."

"Yes, thanks." Jessica paused, looked quickly at the sisters and said, "My son is 9 months old. He needs 10-hour care five days a week." She hesitated. "I'm prepared to discuss the cost and sign a contract." The nuns all nodded in agreement. "I have no difficulty with fees for your service." Again, the nuns all nodded in agreement.

No one other than Mother Superior spoke. "Our care center opens at seven in the morning and closes at six in the evening. All children, whether here for daycare or for adoption, play together, eat together, and attend structured classes according to age. By the way, a child must be nine months old to be accepted into daycare."

"That is fine," Jessica replied.

"Do you have any further questions?"

Jessica cleared her throat, glanced at everyone in the room and said, "How do you know which children are for adoption?"

"Children for adoption wear a red band with their name sewn on their shirt sleeve. It is our policy that every sister assigned to childcare must learn each child's name, identify each, and have knowledge of which child is for adoption. For years now, we've not had any errors. Before you leave, Doctor, Sister Beatrice will give you a tour of the facility." Mother Superior smiled, and Jessica felt much relieved. Stern she might be, but that just meant rules would be followed. Nothing wrong with that.

After the tour, Jessica left feeling she had made the right choice. She would confirm with Cheyenne that she would call her immediately if any emergency occurred while she was caring for Finny in the evening.

Back at her new home, she walked into the bedroom that would become Finny's—the smallest of the three rooms but the prettiest, with teddy-bear and toy wallpaper in red, green and oranges. It made her smile.

Sitting in her recliner, with a cup of Lipton's, she visualized finishing school near year's end. A high-paying job would be in her future. Max had asked her earlier if she'd consider working for him in private practice. It was a tempting offer, but deep down, feelings of uncertainty kept arising. *If I join Max in private practice, will we be compatible? Will we have an equal working partnership? Will I be capable of meeting his high expectations?* Suddenly out of nowhere, a chill swept over her as she realized she still didn't know if he was her rapist. She needed to find out, and soon.

Finishing her drink, Jessica got up and put the glass in the sink. Her thoughts, as always, went back to Silas. Would they ever have a relationship again?

The next Friday by six-thirty in the morning, Jessica was already dressed and on her way to Seattle, her thermos filled with black coffee. The sky was clear and serene, but it was cold. Thinking ahead, she planned a discussion with her mother about Finny's habits and the care he would need. She also needed confirmation from her mother that her apartment and Finny's care would be paid for until her graduation. She felt a little guilty about taking all that money from her mother, particularly since Mother had already been taking care of Finny since his birth, but she reasoned that her mother had plenty of money and assets, so it was probably OK.

More of a problem, however, was that Finny and his grandmother had developed such a strong bond. There had always been conflicts with her mother, and certain strangeness. Would her mother now use her financial power to keep Finny?

It was raining heavily by the time she got to her mother's house. Getting out of the car, she could see that the lawn was immaculately groomed. Like her mother. She knocked gently, and the door opened. Mother stood in the doorway, grinning from ear to ear. Maybe it would be all right.

Jessica entered, gave her mother a hug, and then looked around, hoping to see Finny.

"Can I make you a sandwich? Mother said. You must be hungry and tired. Finny is fast asleep in his crib."

Jessica refrained from dashing into his bedroom. She wanted to be diplomatic: "Mother, can you get him, please? I'd like to see my baby now."

"Certainly, I'll get him." She walked away and returned shortly with Finny in her arms.

"Hi, Finny," Jessica said stroking his forehead while he clung to his grandmother. His big brown eyes opened wide as Jessica plucked him from Mother's arms and showered him with hugs and kisses. He struggled, puckered up his face and screamed annoyance.

"Finny, I'm your mommy." Jessica continued, talking and bouncing him, but to no avail. His arms reached out toward his grandmother, who took him from Jessica and quieted him. She attempted to offer him to Jessica again, but he began crying and clung to her blouse.

"Why don't you leave him here? Mother asked. "He'll have a stable environment, and you'll be graduating within a year."

Jessica's knees threatened to give out, and she sank down on the sofa, inhaling deeply. She had never felt so helpless and trapped in her life. For several long minutes, she stared at her mother. Then, she stood and said, "No, Mother. He needs to be with me. He's mine." Her voice was just short of a shout, her face flushed.

"Mother, my roommate will care for him evenings and whenever necessary. I've made arrangements for day care at a monastery. I'll be able to see Finny daily, and we'll get a chance to finally bond."

After a long discussion, Jessica agreed to stay for two days at her mother's house so that Finny could begin to form an attachment to her. She spent most of the time holding her baby and dancing, singing and playing with him. At the end of the two days, she knew Finny would be upset when he was taken away from his grandmother, but she felt certain he'd adjust after a few more days with her.

She asked her mother for a list of Finny's favorite foods and his sleep schedule. "I'll pack his clothes and playthings tonight and his portable crib in the morning. Is that all right?" she asked. But her mother didn't answer. Instead, she turned away and left the room.

"Mother, please come back here," Jessica whimpered, fighting tears back. "I love you and thank you for everything you've done for Finny and me. I'm only going to Portland, and you can visit as often as you want." Her mother did not respond.

Sunday, Jessica drove back to Portland with Finny strapped into his car seat in back. At the beginning of their trip, he seemed interested in his new surroundings, but as time went on he became restless and unhappy. He banged his rattle against the car seat and threw it on the floor, crying, "Nana! Nana!"

Jessica pulled into the parking lot of a Denny's restaurant near the interstate highway. As she opened the car door, Finny stretched out his arms, face wet with tears and said again, "Nana." She unbuckled the car seat and picked him up. Grabbing her satchel, she carried him into the restaurant. It still felt unfamiliar, having him in her arms, but it felt good. Once in the restaurant, she secured him in a highchair and reached for a cracker in the satchel. Once Finny had the cracker in his hands, he quieted.

The waitress arrived within a few minutes, and Jessica ordered coffee, a small glass of milk, which she poured into his sippy cup, and two bagels. In less than a dozen breaths, Finny began an annoying, whiny cry. People in the restaurant stared at her. One woman even glared at her baby and told her to shut the child up. However, the harder she tried to console Finny, the louder he cried. Finally, she asked the waitress for their order to go, picked her baby up and headed for her car.

After strapping him in his car seat, she simply sat in the car, her hands shaking so violently that she had to grip the key to get it into the ignition. She nearly flooded the engine because her legs were trembling with anger, resentment, and frustration. "What in God's name am I going to do with this kid? Maybe this is a bad idea. Maybe I should go back and leave him with Mother, at least until I graduate." She turned her head, looked at Finny and said, "We'll be home soon, so please stop whimpering." Finny continued to moan intermittently, and then finally drifted off to sleep.

When she arrived at her apartment, Jessica unlocked the door and yelled, "I'm back." She entered carrying Finny who, now that he was awake again, seemed to be fine.

Cheyenne yelled from her bedroom, "That's great. I'll be right out." She entered the living room wide-eyed and wearing a big smile. "Wow!" she said. "Look at this handsome young man."

Jessica put Finny down, and Cheyenne squatted and laughed as he tucked his head behind Jessica's leg. "Finny, I think you and I will be the best of friends."

"I'll be taking the next two days off so I can spend the time with Finny at the monastery while he meets other children." Jessica said.

Cheyenne said she thought that would be a good thing to do.

CHAPTER TWELVE

As Jessica approached the hospital with the cool wind blowing through her still slightly damp hair, she realized how quickly she'd matured. "Doctor" was no longer just a title she wanted to obtain. Somehow, helping people recover from injury and disease had become what she truly wanted. She was proud to soon be a surgeon and now the mother of a soon-to-be 10 month old. She wanted to share her feelings with Silas. She thought he'd appreciate Finny's development. She wanted so much for Silas to accept Finny, whose smile and angelic look would soften any heart.

Thinking about Finny and Silas this morning was what had prompted her to get an early morning start. Her shift didn't begin until the afternoon, which gave her time to go to the research lab. It was still early, 8:15, when she stepped into the lab.

Seth appeared in front of her and said, "Hello, Dr. Tinker. He glanced at the clock on the wall and said, "You've come to work early.

How can I help you?" His voice was businesslike, perhaps aggressive, and his lab coat was wrinkled.

Is he sleep-deprived or just annoyed that I'm here? Jessica wondered. "I'd like to speak with Dr. Rolland."

"Just one moment, I'll see if he's in back."

Jessica hoped that Silas wouldn't ask her to leave. She moved toward the window to wait. Several people walked in and out of the laboratory. Dr. Gunner walked in and began talking with the receptionist. Ten more minutes passed. She turned to go, and at that point Silas appeared from around the corner. "What can I do for you, Jessica?" he asked coldly.

"Good morning, Silas." She was surprised that he'd addressed her as Jessica. "Can we talk?"

"No," he said. "Not here. Not now. Jessica, that's no reason to barge in here without calling. I'm very busy. What do you want?" His voice cut her to the bone.

"I had to come here. You never call. Silas…" Her hands were shaking.

Silas turned away and walked over to Seth. Jessica saw him shake his head as if in disgust, and then he turned and walked past her out the door. "Let's go for coffee for a few minutes," he said abruptly. As they left, Jessica saw Dr. Gunner entering Seth's office, and wondered about the purpose of his visit with Seth so early in the morning.

She walked with Silas to the coffee shop in silence. The place was practically empty, and she was thankful for that.

"Silas, I'm here to let you know that I love you, and I am asking for a second chance to work on our relationship. That is, if you still love me?"

The waitress appeared, stood at the end of the table, and said, "Are you ready to order?"

"Yes," Silas replied firmly. "I'll have coffee and French toast."

"I'll have black coffee."

The waitress nodded and walked off.

"Now, Jessie, what is it that you want?" He said, as though she hadn't just told him what she wanted. Staring into his eyes, eyes that always seemed to be seeing a part of her no one else could see, she said, "I'm asking for a second chance to work on our relationship." She paused, and then said, "I'm asking you to accept my son, too. He is a beautiful, innocent child. What do you think?"

"Jessie, you fooled me into believing your lies. I don't trust you anymore. I don't know if I'll ever be able to again, or if I'll ever be able to accept your child by another man."

"Silas, everyone makes mistakes. Is there no forgiveness in your heart?"

"Just cut that crap, all right? This is so like you. You try to add a little excitement to your shameful life, and then, when it all hits the fan, you come running for forgiveness. When you told me about your rape a long time ago, I wanted to kill the man who did that to you. But this… this… a child, well…" He paused, looked at her, and then said, "Yes, Jessie, I still love you, but I don't know if I can forgive you. Maybe we can just be friends. That's all I want right now, nothing more."

"Fine. Thanks for having coffee with me." Jessica placed two one-dollar bills next to her coffee cup, stood, and said, "Thanks again for your time, Silas. I'll think about what you said. Hopefully, there will never be a time when you make a terrible mistake." She turned, walked out of the coffee shop, and got into her car.

Jessica went home, dashed into the kitchen, and made herself a strong drink. She gulped it down and fixed another. Trying to relax in the recliner, she let the tears flow. She looked around the room, then, her eyes became focused on an 8X10-framed picture of Silas and her, posing cheek-to-cheek. A thought popped into her head, *I wonder if Mother still has a copy of this photo?*

When the glass was empty again, she looked at her watch. It was nearly noon and she was starved. She made herself a third drink and decided to make a sandwich. She opened the fridge, and much to her surprise found it full of fresh produce instead of sandwich makings. Cheyenne had done some shopping. Finny would enjoy homemade vegetable soup. *It's important to prepare nutritious meals for him,* she thought. *If only I can find the time to do it.*

Jessica decided to drive to the hospital cafeteria for lunch. Driving was difficult, though. Her vision was fuzzy, and the car seemed to veer left and right of its own volition. She rolled down the windows, took deep breaths of fresh air, and was feeling safer when she saw flashing lights behind her. She pulled over, hands shaking, and waited.

The officer approached her window and said, "You crossed the center line several times." He held his right hand over his holster and ordered, "Your driver's license and car registration, please." He watched her intently as she complied. When he had the papers in hand, she said, "Officer, I've been preoccupied. I'm on my way to surgery—an emergency case." Her heart was thumping against her rib cage. She felt fortunate that she'd opened the car windows earlier.

"Ms. Tinker, wait here." The officer turned and went back to his car to check her criminal record.

Thank God I don't have a record, she thought. *Then, I can't be arrested for DUI, I just can't.*

In a few minutes, the officer returned, handed her the papers and said, "I'm not going to issue a ticket this time, but this is a warning," he sounded disgusted. "Drive carefully and pay attention." He turned and left. Jessica sat there for a minute or two, taking deep breaths to regain her composure and get a grip on what she'd done. The outcome could've been disastrous.

When she arrived at the cafeteria, Max was sitting alone, enjoying lunch. He looked up and said, "Jessica, are you all right? You're glassy-eyed and somewhat unsteady on your feet. Have you been drinking?"

"Yes, Max" She sat down, uninvited. "And five minutes ago, a policeman pulled me over for zigzagging. Luckily, he only gave me a warning. But Max, I lied. I told him I had an emergency case."

"Don't worry about it. Did you have anything to eat?"

"I'm really not hungry."

"That's not the point. You need to eat something."

Jessica looked over at his plate and said, "What are you eating?"

"Sirloin steak, veggies, and salad. I'm drinking water." He grinned.

When the waitress approached the table, Jessica said, "I'll have a hamburger patty, veggies, and salad. Water to drink."

"That's my girl," Max said.

Jessica ate a few bites of her meal and stopped. "I'm full."

"Finish your meal." Max addressed her with firmness, but around his eyes, lines crinkled as if he was about to laugh. He said nothing at all then, just continued with that smile, until she finished her meal. It took an hour, after which she felt much better. Then, he insisted upon paying for both of them.

"Thanks for your kindness and the meal. I should have you over for dinner sometime soon." Jessica smiled, stood up steady, and walked out the door before Max could respond.

CHAPTER THIRTEEN

Jessica parked her car at a city meter and got out in front of the Marriott Hotel in downtown Portland. It was nippy, the evening breeze cool and moist—May in Oregon. She looked at her watch. It was nearly 6:30, and she was starved. Her mother had said she would order room service for the two of them. She said she was exhausted from shopping and her flight from Seattle. A quiet dinner was just what she wanted.

Jessica rode the elevator to the fifth floor, wondering why her mother thought it best to stay at a hotel rather than sleep in a bed in her daughter's apartment. This would be the first time the two of them had seen each other since she'd gone to Seattle to get Finny, and she wasn't sure her mother's mood would be any more positive now than it had been then. She knocked on the door in some trepidation, but when it opened her mother was smiling.

"Come in, come in." Mother peered around Jessica. "Are you alone?"

"Yes, Mother, who else did you expect?"

"Actually, I thought perhaps Silas would come with you." She paused before adding quickly, "But that was just a thought. Now, come here and let me hug you."

After they hugged, her mother looked Jessica over and said, "Honey, you look exhausted, but I guess you're just busy. How is that grandson of mine?" Her voice was just a touch plaintive.

"Mother, I'm sure you miss Finny tremendously. Tomorrow, we can visit him most of the morning at the monastery. The sisters are kind, loving, and provide a sense of stability for him. He also gets to interact with many other children."

"When do you see him?" Her mother's now seemed irritated.

"As often as possible. Right now he's at home with Cheyenne. She's in her second year of medical school. You'd like her. Do you really have to leave for Seattle in a day? I'm having a small get-together this weekend in celebration of Finny's first birthday. Are you sure you can't stay?"

"I can't. Your stepfather isn't well. He's undergoing a series of studies to rule out cancer. I'm really worried about him. I flew here today because I had urgent financial business to deal with. I have to get back to him, but I'll see Finny tomorrow before I leave."

"Mother, I hope your husband gets better." Jessica cleared her throat. "I'll pick you up early tomorrow morning." She thought it was odd that her mother could fly here on financial business but could not come to Finny's birthday party, but there was little point in mentioning this. Maybe her mother had still not forgiven her for taking Finny to Portland?

At the crack of dawn the next day, Jessica showered, dressed, and made Finny's breakfast. Then she stepped into his bedroom. He looked at her, eyes sparkling, blowing bubbles and drooling. She scooped him up, kissed him, and then washed his face, combed his thick brown hair, changed his diaper, and put him in a pair of navy corduroy pants and a shirt. After breakfast, the two left for the monastery.

When they arrived, several children had already been dropped off. Jessica kissed and hugged Finny and told him, "Mommy will be right back with Grandma." One of the sisters then took him over to play with the other children.

Jessica drove to the Marriott Hotel, dashed into the elevator, and got off on the fifth floor. She inhaled deeply and knocked on the door. When her mother opened the door, she said, "Mother, are you ready? I think Finny will be happy to see you."

"Won't you step in?" her mother said. "I'm all packed. After seeing Finny, I'll leave for Seattle. But now, give me a minute to get myself together and put some lipstick on."

Jessica wasn't in an argumentative mood, so she waited patiently for her mother to get ready. After 25 minutes, though, she began pacing. Finally, she stepped toward the bathroom door, hesitated for a second wondering if she should knock, then tapped softly and said, "Mother, is everything okay?"

"Yes, honey, I'll be right out."

Her mother stepped into the sitting area looking somber. As usual, she was dressed in the latest style: a white fitted shirt, a red silk scarf and a narrow, black-striped skirt with a matching jacket. She had styled her hair in a frizz.

Jessica realized her mother was hurting and covering up her pain with her perfect ensemble and careful makeup. Feeling guilty, she stepped toward her mother and took her into her arms. "Mother, I do love you and appreciate everything you've done for me all these years. I hope one day to repay you for all your kindness and help. And I know Finny is important to you. Remember, you can see him anytime you wish."

"You don't need to repay anything. Now let's go and visit my grandson." Jessica could see that her mother was still resenting her taking Finny with her before she had completed her residency. On their way out, her mother grabbed a large shopping bag filled with wrapped packages.

"Mother, what are you bringing to the monastery? The sisters have strict rules and regulations. There is no favoritism among the children."

"This is something special. Wait and see."

When they arrived at the monastery, Jessica said, "Mother, we have to wait for a sister to come and get us." The two women sat on a padded wooden bench, and Jessica leaned her head back against the wall, closed her eyes, and took in some long, quiet breaths. A sister appeared within a few minutes, and Jessica introduced her mother. She and her mother followed the sister down a hallway, and in seconds, her mother had spotted Finny sitting on the carpeted floor playing with a toy truck. There were two other children nearby, also playing. Her mother handed the sister the shopping bag and dashed toward Finny, scooped him up, and inundated him with kisses. Finny didn't object, exactly, but he did struggle to be put down.

"Mommy," he said, reaching for Jessica.

"Finny, it's Grandma. Come give me a hug." Mother reached for him, but Finny waddled toward his mother. Jessica picked him up and said, "This is your grandma. She loves you a lot."

"He should have stayed with me. He doesn't even know who I am." Her mother's voice was harsh. She stared at Jessica.

"Mother, he doesn't understand. He's just a baby."

Mother ignored her, looked around and approached the Sister standing near a window. She said, "Sister, the shopping bag I handed you is filled with wrapped toys appropriate for children of different ages." She then turned and walked toward Jessica and said, "Let's go."

As they were leaving, the Sister handed Jessica's mother a big, khaki envelope, the kind that closes by wrapping a little string around a little button.

"What is this?" Mother took the envelope and glared at the nun.

The Sister replied, "Please read the information and take the shopping bag filled with packages with you."

"No! I will not. These are for the children. Distribute them. But if you don't, then throw them in the garbage." She looked at her daughter. "I'm ready to leave." Her eyes were wide and her face crimson.

On the way to the Marriott Hotel, Mother sat in the car, pouting. Without saying a word, she pulled out a small, round mirror from her purse, applied lipstick, checked her teeth, and pulled a few strands of hair into position. Next, she opened the envelope the sister gave her, scanned it quickly, and said, "This is a waste of paper. I don't need to review their rules and regulations." She flung the papers into the back seat. "These nuns are rigid, inconsiderate and—might I add—selfish." Mother turned and shot Jessica an icy glare.

Jessica applied the brake. "Mother, please calm down. You're jumping to conclusions." For a while, there was silence. Then Jessica suggested they have a quick lunch at the Chart House, to which her mother responded with a curt nod.

The restaurant was packed when they arrived but fortunately, the wait time was short. They were seated in a cramped corner, and Mother didn't complain but glanced around the restaurant. The waitress arrived at their table and took their order. Suddenly, Jessica saw her mother's face go pale. She had put her hand over her heart.

"Mother, are you having a heart attack?" Jessica asked.

"No, but you won't believe this. I think I see Silas behind you. He's with a woman, a pretty blonde, in the far corner."

Jessica turned, looked, and said, "She looks familiar. Probably one of the hospital's nurses. Silas and I are no longer seeing each other," she stated firmly, almost coldly.

Somehow they got through lunch, after which Jessica drove to the Marriott Hotel, parked and said, "Mother, thanks for coming to see Finny. Next time you visit, he'll be a bit more mature." She paused and added, "I love you."

Her mother stepped out of the car and wished Jessica well in school and with Finny's care.

Jessica's last words were rushed and slightly loud. "Mother, Finny loves you. He just needs time to grow older and understand who you are."

CHAPTER FOURTEEN

Saturday by 6:30 p.m. Jessica's friends and their children had left her apartment following a brief celebration of Finny's slightly overdue first birthday. The party was subdued but pleasant.

Jessica and Finny had eaten dinner. He was bathed, dressed in his new pair of pajamas, and ready for bed. She held him on her lap in the recliner and read to him. For about half the story, he giggled as she read, adding his inflections and expressions to her voice. She had timed it right: by the end of the story, he was asleep. She kissed him and carried him into his crib, then mixed some vodka and orange juice and nestled comfortably in her recliner.

Mother was never far from her mind, and tonight she was in the forefront. *Mother is an intelligent woman,* she thought. *She would be able to raise Finny well, but my baby is* my *baby, not hers. Surely, Mother will eventually accept that, and stop holding a grudge against me. Until that time, there's nothing I can do about her distress. But I can, and must do, something about her bad-mannered behavior toward the nun at the monastery. I'll apologize to the nun on Monday.*

Then there was graduation. Because she's been absent during her pregnancy, she wouldn't finish her classes until late fall. Then what? She thought about Max. *What will it be like working with him? Will Mother be willing to loan me money so I can become an equal partner if Max establishes a private practice?*

The phone rang, snapping her out of her reverie. She stood, walked to the kitchen, and picked up the receiver.

It was a very upbeat Leslie. "Hey! Alex and I are hosting a party this weekend. Hope you can come. Be here about three o'clock next Saturday. Oh, and bring Silas. I haven't seen him awhile. Also, I have news: I'm going to return to obstetrical and gynecological private group practice downtown, starting next month! I'm excited and eager to be getting back to being something, other than somebody's mother."

Jessica interrupted. "What about the kids?

"Oh, they're going to be in kindergarten. We hired a great baby sitter, but either Alex or I will be home every evening, so we'll be able to spend time with them. Alex is starting up his own law firm."

Jessica couldn't very well bring Silas, but she wondered if he would come to the party and, if so, whether he would bring the blonde she'd seen him with at the Chart House.

The day of the party was a glorious, crisp afternoon. Jessica arrived half an hour early so she could tell Leslie about what had happened to her relationship with Silas. She rapped on the door and Alex appeared.

"Hi, Jessica. Come on in. Leslie's in the kitchen."

She had just stepped into the foyer when Leslie appeared. "Hey,

Jessica, come give me a hand in the kitchen. What's new these days?"

"Nothing, really." Jessica swallowed hard and said, "I want you to know that Silas and I aren't seeing each another anymore." Then she suddenly burst into tears.

"Oh, my God, what happened? He said nothing when I invited him to our party."

"Excuse me, I need to sit down. Could you get me a glass of water?" Jessica said. Leslie obliged and pulled up chairs for them both.

"I want you to keep the information I'm going to tell you in confidence." Leslie nodded, and Jessica continued, "I have a son."

Leslie moved her chair closer and placed her arm around Jessica's shoulder. Taken aback, she didn't know what to say, but after a long silence, she said, "I don't understand. When did this happen? Why didn't you tell me?"

After Jessica dried her eyes, she said, "My son just turned a year old. His name is Finny, and he is the sweetest child. I didn't tell you because Silas is not the father, and I was ashamed of what I had done. Now, Silas can't accept my son or me after what I did, despite the fact that I still love him."

"What the hell were you thinking? Who's the father?"

"It's a long story, Leslie. Maybe one day we can talk about it. In the meantime, please keep this a secret."

"I promise."

"Thanks for listening."

"I'm happy for you. One day soon, I'd like to meet your son."

"You will."

Guests started arriving. There were a few new faces, but Jessica knew most of them, though she'd not seen them in quite a while. She had stopped coming to Leslie's parties when she found out she was pregnant with Finny.

Glad I'm not pregnant now, she thought as she sat down at the bar and poured herself a glass of wine. As she sipped, she admired the room just off the kitchen. It was decorated in exquisite taste.

Jessica was refilling her glass when she heard a male voice. It was Max. Her heart began to pound. He stepped up beside her and eyed the wine bottle on the bar.

"Can I pour you a glass?" she asked quickly.

"A Merlot, thanks." He smiled. He had stubble on his face, and as usual, his thick hair went its own way despite being combed.

"I had a hell of a case this morning, an auto accident. Three young people were hurt." He took a big swig.

"You must be exhausted."

"I am, but all I want is food, wine, and a good friend." Max winked and made eye contact with her.

Just then, Gunner walked into the room. He was wearing his wrinkled, thousand-dollar tweed jacket and a frown on his face.

He stepped toward Max and said, "What kind of surgery were you two up to this morning?" He glared at Jessica for a moment and then looked back at Max. "How did your pony-tailed assistant do?" He laughed aloud— a hateful and mean laughter.

"For your information, Karl, it wasn't Dr. Tinker who assisted me this morning." But Dr. Gunner persisted. He refilled his wine glass, shifted his posture, and said, "Wasn't she up to the task?"

Max became angry. His face flushed, and he said, "Karl, you've had enough to drink. Why don't you back off Jessica and leave her alone?"

"What is this, a conspiracy?" Gunner yelled. He walked away, his gait somewhat wobbly.

"Thank you very much for coming to my rescue, Max. He's always picking on me. I really think he has a deep-seated hang-up against women—against me."

Max didn't respond to this. Instead, consulted his wristwatch and said, "I'm going to try some of this delicious-looking food and attempt to socialize. Why don't you join me?"

Jessica surveyed the buffet table and took a donut, but then decided to add a salad and veggies. Max made a huge sandwich. They sat together on a small sofa holding their plates on their laps; Jessica taking dainty party-manner type bites, and Max, on the other hand opening his mouth like a fish to fit the sandwich in. Jessica laughed. Taking an even larger bite, he chewed laboriously, swallowed and wiped his mouth with a napkin. Then he took a long swig of his wine. Jessica watched, tracing her index finger down the sweat on the outside of her wine glass.

"It's really good. Here, have a bite." He offered her his sandwich.

"Thanks, but I've got plenty on my plate." Jessica cleared her throat and said, "I'd like to invite you to dinner at my place next Sunday. Remember, a while ago, I said I'd invite you to a home-cooked meal."

"Yeah, I recall you saying that. I wondered if you'd actually do it."

"I always keep my word." She eyed him with a big grin. "How about you come over around four o'clock? You don't have any food allergies, do you?"

"No allergies. And four o'clock sounds good. Should I bring anything?"

"Just yourself." Jessica smiled widely while considering whether the decision to invite Max over would come back to bite her. Thoughts arose unbidden about how she could check his shoulder for tattoos.

They both stood, and Jessica walked into the kitchen and placed her plate on the sink. When she turned, she saw Leslie in the living room talking to Silas and a blonde woman. The woman's wavy blonde hair was cut short. Jessica guessed her age at about 30. She was thin, almost gaunt, and had a smile that seemed plastered on her face. Jessica thought she might be the same woman he had been with in the Chart House, but she wasn't sure. She wondered if the woman was a medical professional of some sort.

Leslie seemed to have noticed the dwindling supply of food on the table. She dashed into the kitchen and started refilling all the plates and bowls that were laid out. As she worked, she turned to Jessica and said, "Silas addressed the woman as his friend. I didn't ask about her profession."

A few minutes later, Silas and the woman approached the food table and filled their plates. As Silas turned, Jessica walked past him and said, "Hi Silas."

He acknowledged her with a smile and said, "Hi, Jessie."

Jessica kept walking and stopped next to Dr. Stout, who was engaged in a conversation with Seth, Leslie's husband Alexander, and his legal assistant. Jessica tried to listen for a few minutes to their conversation, but realized she wasn't hearing a word of what they were saying.

Unexpectedly, a hand touched her shoulder. She looked to her right and said, "Dr. Stout, I'm sorry, my mind was wandering."

"You're like me—a ton of material floating around in your head," Dr. Stout chuckled.

Jessica thanked him for understanding and left the conversation, stepping out onto the deck. She joined Max, who said, "I need to thank you for being such an understanding person, Jessica, and I appreciate your invitation to dinner." He gave her a hug. "I'm about to leave. Take care. I'll probably see you tomorrow at the hospital."

She watched him walk away, and then she turned and became aware of Silas watching her. Mute with jealousy and anger, she ignored him and moved about the room.

Suddenly, Alexander tapped his wine glass with a spoon and said, "Ladies and gentlemen." He paused, smiled and continued, "Leslie and I hosted this party first to celebrate Leslie's return to her practice." He paused again, "And second, because I've opened a private law firm. There are five attorneys in my firm. I think we'll all stay very busy."

Leslie then added, "Please refer me to all your friends and their friends who are pregnant, or plan on starting a family. And now, everyone, please raise your glasses, and let's toast to success."

Everyone said, "To success!" and drank deeply.

Jessica approached Leslie and said, "This was a great party, but I have to leave now. Unfortunately, Cheyenne has plans for late tonight, and I need to get back to Finny."

Leslie thanked her for coming, and Jessica left, managing to avoid meeting the blonde, or engaging in conversation with Silas.

CHAPTER FIFTEEN

The sky was cloudless and dazzling on an early Monday morning in June. Jessica was relieved to see the sun shining through the bedroom window, making her feel optimistic about starting the day on a happy note. She gave little thought to Leslie and Alexander's party the night before, concentrating instead on planning a dinner menu for Max next Sunday. She thought she'd consult Cheyenne. Perhaps she'd have suggestions for a home-cooked meal.

Getting out of bed, she made her way into the bathroom to shower. Then she fed Finny, dressed him and dropped him off at the day care before heading to the hospital. There, she made patient rounds and consulted with her preceptor, after which she spent the remainder of the morning in the medical library.

When her pager beeped, she hesitated before answering. She wanted to ignore it, but it might be an emergency. A glance told her it was the research center calling. Why would she be needed in the research center? She got to the nearest phone, dialed the number and said, "Dr. Tinker speaking. You paged me?"

"Jessie, thank you for calling back so quickly." She recognized Silas's voice on the other end of the line. "Sorry for bothering you, but I'd like to take you to a matinee this afternoon. Is that possible?"

This was odd. He had continually snubbed her since their breakup. Jessica wondered what he really wanted. "What's the occasion?" she asked.

"I don't have time to discuss it now, but are you interested? And do you have the time?"

"Yes, Silas, I'll go. What time is this matinee, and where do we meet?"

"I'll pick you up at your place at three. Is that all right?"

"Yes."

They hung up. Jessica was confused. *All that time cold, aloof, curt,* she thought. *Now he's being nice. Or was he? Something about his voice had seemed ... angry.* Well, she'd find out what was going on soon enough. She rushed home, ate a sandwich and put on jeans, a v-neck lilac shirt and a pair of well-worn loafers.

At three o'clock, there was a rap on the door.

"Silas? Is that you?"

"Yes!" a firm voice called from the other side. "Are you ready, Jessie?"

"Yes." She grabbed her satchel from the sofa and opened the door.

When they arrived at the theatre, Jessica asked, "Which movie are we seeing?"

"An old movie, *La Cage aux Folles*," Silas said.

Why a comedy when they were both having difficulty dealing with pain and loneliness after their failed relationship? A movie that would relieve those pent-up feelings might have been more appropriate. She sat through it patiently, even though it made her feel awful. She wanted to get up and leave. Jessica wanted even more to find out what was going on with Silas. So she was glad after the movie when he asked if she'd like to have a coffee. "We can talk," he said.

Silas and Jessica walked to a restaurant near the theatre. The place was crowded, but they were able to find a small table. They ordered coffee and strawberry shortcake.

A silence ensued. Silas finally broke it. "Jessie, Dr. Brown seemed terribly chummy with you at Leslie's party. What was that all about?"

"For heaven's sake, Silas. He's my preceptor and a brilliant thoracic surgeon. You'd like him. He's a great teacher."

"I bet he is," Silas said. Was he actually jealous? After rejecting her?

"What about you? What's the story with your blonde?"

"Oh, her? The lady you saw me with is one of the assistants in the administration department and, to some extent, is responsible for the finances in research. She's good company, but she doesn't replace you," Silas replied.

For a long time, neither spoke nor moved. Jessica's heart raced and pounded in her chest. *Never in my life have I felt such anger radiate from a person, even though he's trying to disguise it with smiles while acting nonchalant,* she thought.

Finally, Silas said, "I've tried over and over to accept your betrayal and your baby. I can't trust you anymore, but I believe we can remain friends. We'll see each other at the hospital and on other occasions, and since you're interested in research, we can meet from time to time and discuss the latest trials. What do you think?"

"Remember the comment I made to you awhile back? About you never making mistakes? I hope you'll think about that in the future."

"Jessie, just out of curiosity, is Max the father of your child?"

"Why? That's none of your business! It's also irrelevant," she said, her voice cracking and getting louder. She glared at him.

After that, there was an attempt at some small talk, which didn't resolve any of their differences. They parted with an aloof embrace.

CHAPTER SIXTEEN

Friday afternoon following work, Jessica cleaned the house, shopped, and prepared some food ahead of time. Sunday, her day off, allowed time for relaxation since Max wasn't going to arrive until the afternoon. Cheyenne's parents were arriving in Portland for a visit, but they were staying at a hotel, giving Jessica plenty of time to spend with Finny.

Jessica looked over the suggested recipes from Cheyenne's mother and decided to make chicken a la champagne, twice-baked potato, carrots, peas, green beans, and French apple cake for dessert. Her dinner wouldn't be flashy, but she still hoped it would impress Max. *Relax,* she reminded herself. *Just be you.*

Jessica spent quite a lot of time in the kitchen when Sunday arrived. She had dinner ready a few minutes before four o'clock when Max arrived, holding a huge bouquet of flowers. "Hi," he said. "These are for you."

"Thank you. What a beautiful bouquet." Her heart soared. She hadn't expected flowers.

Max looked debonair in jeans, a light blue shirt, and a tweed jacket with leather patches on the elbows.

"I need to put these in water. Would you mind pouring the wine?" she asked as she handed him a bottle. "The glasses are over there," she said, pointing.

A tantalizing aroma wafted from the kitchen as Max poured. He inhaled deeply and said, "Whatever you're cooking sure smells good." He watched Jessica open the oven and pull out a sheet of golden-brown biscuits.

"May I?" He extended his arm and picked up a biscuit as she was transferring them onto a plate. Grabbing a bit of butter off the butter dish on the counter, he spread a generous dollop between the layers of biscuit, took a bite, and said, "Delicious."

"Dinner will be ready in a jiffy," she said. "But first, I have something important to tell you. Please sit down." She gestured to the couch in the living room.

Max took his glass of wine, sat down, and said, "Shoot."

"Max." She paused, almost overcome with shame, and then blurted, "I have a child." Ignoring the astounded look on Max's face, she continued, "He's napping in the next room." Her mouth twitched as she spoke, and she shuddered. "I was stupid, and I had a brief affair with a married man, not knowing he was married."

Max interrupted softly, "You're still in love with this man?"

"No, no, I was never in love. Just momentarily infatuated and half drunk. I really know nothing about him. I only saw him a couple of times."

Max stared at her for a long time. Finally, he smiled, scooted closer toward her and rubbed his fingers along his jaw. He said, "Wow, I wish I didn't like you so damn much." He put his arm around her shoulder and gave her a squeeze.

Jessica smiled. "I like you, too, Max."

"You shouldn't. I'm nothing but trouble to a great surgeon like you, Jessica."

"Do you really think I'm a great surgeon?" she asked, immensely pleased.

"The best. And I've been around for some time." He lifted his gaze from his glass, his eyes held a mischievous twinkle, and his boyish grin was in place.

At that moment, Finny began yelling, "Mommy!"

"Excuse me. I'll be just a second."

Jessica ran into her son's bedroom, scooped him up, changed his diaper and said, "I'd like you to meet Mommy's friend."

She turned and the baby cooed at Max, who was leaning against the bedroom door.

Max smiled at Finny and said, "Hi, big boy." He turned to Jessica and said, "He has your mouth, and maybe a hint of your hair color."

"I think he's the spitting image of his father, but it's hard to predict what he'll look like in the future. But he does have my personality." She was proud of her son and proud of herself, too.

They stepped into the dining room, and Jessica put Finny in his high chair.

"Max, would you dig out a couple of toys from Finny's toy box for him to play with while I get the food on the table?"

"Consider it done." Max handed Finny a toy and played hide and seek around his high chair, Finny giggled, drooled with excitement, and banged his toy on the tray.

In a few minutes, the food was set out on the table, and Jessica joined them. Max sat in a chair next to Finny. Jessica sat to Finny's right and put a bib around his neck. The sun streamed through the window and lit up his dark hair.

Jessica bowed her head and said a short prayer. Looking up at Max, she said, "Please help yourself to everything." She offered Finny baby food and mashed table food. From time to time, Max would make funny faces or snap his fingers, and Finny would stare at him and smile from ear to ear.

After dinner, Max helped with the dishes and then lay on the floor and laughed while Finny crawled all over him.

Jessica looked at her watch and said, "Finny, it's time for your bath." She extended her arms to pick up her son. But Finny ran to Max, and clung to a pant leg. Max scooped him up, hugged and kissed him on the cheek, and said, "Hey, big boy, your mommy wants to bathe you." Finny put his arms around Max's neck, refusing to budge. Max lifted him high above his head and twirled him several times—and Finny, staring at Max wide-eyed, vomited on the man's shirt.

Jessica rushed to apologize, but Max insisted that no harm was done. "I should not have twirled him after his meal." He removed his shirt and said, "Finny, you little rascal. Now, we both have to take a bath."

"You can use my shower," Jessica said, pointing to her bedroom. Max thanked her, turned and hurried into the bathroom. As he turned, Jessica got a glorious glimpse of his bare shoulders—no bald eagle tattoo! She felt like jumping for joy.

While Max was in the shower, Jessica bathed Finny in a small tub in the guest bathroom, put clean pajamas on him and tucked him into bed. She was back in the living room, hardly able to contain her delight, when Max came back in, a bath towel wrapped around his neck. He was wearing his pants, but he held his shirt in his hand.

"I haven't had this much fun in years, Jessica," he said. They both laughed. "I'll put your shirt in the wash," Jessica said, realizing that she was so excited that she was faltering a bit and her words were slurred.

Max, with a puzzled glance at her, said, "Jessica, I want to thank you for the superb home-cooked meal. I think your son is simply wonderful. I wish I had a son like that." He stopped abruptly. With a furrowed brow, he said, "Maybe one day." He paused again. "I should escape from the prison of work and become more diversified. You know, I think I need a bit more fun in my life."

Her heart skittered. "Yes." She felt renewed hope and determination as she looked at him. "Would you like another glass of wine?" she asked, hoping he would agree.

"Since my shirt is in the wash, I don't see why not."

Jessica refilled his glass and got them both a slice of French apple pie a la mode. The phone rang just as they were settling down on the sofa. Jessica hesitated but did get up to answer it. "Hello."

"Hey, it's Cheyenne. I'm calling to let you know I'll be home late. My parents and I have lots to do." Cheyenne said excitedly.

"That's fine. Have fun!" Jessica replied cheerfully.

When Jessica hung up and returned to the living room, Max said, "The washer buzzed, so I put the clothes in the dryer."

"Thank you," she replied. They both returned and sat on the sofa.

"This cake goes well with the wine," he said, shifting closer to Jessica.

"Yes, it's tasty, and the wine is just right."

As they talked about the future, Max turned to face Jessica--and then he kissed her. And she returned his kiss.

After a while, the dryer buzzed. Max kissed her once again and then said, "You're a good kisser."

"Gee, so are you," she replied with a megawatt smile.

The interlude interrupted, Jessica retrieved Max's shirt from the dryer. He put it on, saying how good it felt to put it on still warm from the dryer. "By the way," he said, "where does Finny stay during your working hours?"

"Cheyenne and I look after him evenings and weekends. During the weekdays, he stays at the Order of Holy Sanctuary Monastery until evening." *Why this interest?* she wondered.

"Oh, the monastery!" Max said. "Hey, if you're free on Wednesday, I'd love to go to the monastery with you when you pick him up. I'd be interested in touring the place."

"Sure. When I pick Finny up Monday, I'll ask the sisters if it's possible to give us a tour. They also provide care for children up for adoption." Jessica told him she was impressed with the care Finny was receiving, and had recommended the monastery to Leslie since her kids would need after-school care. "Leslie had been so impressed," Jessica said, "that she was planning to refer patients there, either for daycare or for adoption."

After a while of talking, Max said, "Jessica, it's getting late, and I do need to go. I've a busy day tomorrow. See you Wednesday." He put his arms around her, gave her a squeeze, and then kissed her long and hard.

That Wednesday afternoon, Max showed up late. "Sorry I'm late," he apologized, "but surgery took longer than I thought. There were complications. Oh, did you say the monastery care center closes at seven?"

"Yes. We need to hurry."

"Fine, let's take my car since it's parked in front of the apartment building."

"Okay," She only hoped they had enough time.

It was 5:45 when they arrived. A sister met them in the entryway. Jessica had seen her only a time or two. She was young and pretty.

"Sister, my name is Dr. Tinker, and this is Dr. Brown. I called earlier and arranged for a tour of the care facility. I'm also here to pick my son up from daycare."

"I'm Sister Ellen, and I'll take you folks on a quick tour. To begin, this is the kitchen where our nutritious meals are prepared." The sister showed them sleeping quarters, nap rooms and play areas before stopping and pointing. "And this is the sick room." The walls in this area were beautifully decorated in cheerful, warm colors, and there were pictures on the wall.

Suddenly, Max came to a stop in front of a large framed portrait. With a look of wonder on his face, he asked, "Any particular reason why Dr. Gunner's photo is here?"

Sister Ellen replied respectfully, "This gentleman is on our board. He oversees all activities so far as the children are concerned. He helps draw up the adoption rules."

"He's not even a Catholic." Max whispered into Jessica's ear.

Sister Ellen checked a small watch and announced that the center would be closing soon. Max and Jessica thanked her, and Jessica went to get Finny.

At the car, Jessica remembered she hadn't brought Finny's car seat. "No problem," Max said. "Hold him on your lap, and I'll take the shortest route to your apartment. We'll get his car seat and go to a restaurant for dinner. Finny can throw some food around." He grinned.

Glancing at him, Jessica realized that Max would always be delightful to be around. He was just who he was, no pretense. When he smiled, crinkles formed around his eyes like little canyons, the depths of the wrinkles slightly tanned from the wind and sun, revealing his extra time spent outdoors.

The car seat was fetched, and Max put Finny into it, ruffling his hair.

At the restaurant, Max asked Jessica what she knew about Gunner's position on the monastery board. "He's always complaining about how much time it takes to be a member of the hospital board, chief of surgery, and a teacher, always implying the world owes him a living. How in God's name did he get that position?" Max seemed puzzled.

"Well, Max, I think he's a power fanatic. I actually believe he would go to the nth degree to obtain power and money. He just seems so greedy, so it would be unlikely this would be charity."

"I don't know, but I'll keep an open mind about this."

"Max, please don't mention to Dr. Gunner that Finny goes to daycare at the monastery."

"He doesn't know?"

"No, he doesn't."

"Alright. I promise that'll be our secret." He laughed again and tousled her hair.

CHAPTER SEVENTEEN

The following Wednesday, Jessica sat at a desk near a window in the library staring outside. Maple trees swayed gently in the breeze as she rocked her pencil between her middle and index fingers. Her mind was a million miles away, wondering if Silas even gave a damn whether she lived or died. He did seem pleased with his accomplishments. He was knee deep in drug trials, the lab was his safe haven, and his boss was consumed by his obsession with research and curing disease. Jessica, too, had always been intrigued by research, but with Silas in the lab, she would never consider working there. But their relationship seemed to be at an end, permanently. She felt so rejected.

She compared Max to Silas. Max was smart, motivated, and had a great sense of humor. Most of all, he liked and accepted Finny. Jessica was fond of Max, and she knew he admired her and was fond of her, as well. She hoped that, after graduation and board certification, she could practice alongside him. She felt so much better about herself lately, knowing that Max valued her as competent and assertive, rather than just as someone of the opposite gender.

Rustling sounds from behind a bookshelf snapped her back to reality. She refocused on the text in front of her. But the rustling sound continued, making her curious. She glanced over at the sound – and spotted Silas no more than 20 feet away flipping pages in a text.

"Hi, Silas. What are you doing here?" she asked in what she hoped was a neutral tone.

"Hi, Jessie." Silas beamed like a kid who'd finished his homework early. "I was thinking about calling you to let you know that Seth and I are now in the midst of the drug clinical trial with the rabbits. Do you have time to stop by the lab—see your favorite white rabbits? Seth will be leaving for the day."

"Sure. I'd like to see how the trial is going."

They both stood. Silas waited for Jessica to step in front of him before following her out of the library. On their way to the lab, they stepped into the coffee shop and ordered coffee to go.

Arriving at the lab, Jessica approached the rabbit cages. Suddenly, a loud noise echoed across the room. She and Silas peeked around the corner and saw Seth smashing his fist again on his desk, then wincing at the pain. He rubbed his knuckles and stared at the two of them.

"It upsets me when Gunner continues to nag me about drug-trial details," he said by way of explanation. "I told him, 'No more of this nagging and prying bullshit.' I don't care if he's on the board or not!"

Silas ran his fingers through his hair, seemingly lost for words. Jessica just stood motionless with her mouth hanging open. *Is Seth saying what I think he's saying?* she thought. *Or did I not hear him correctly?*

"Jessica, what are you doing here?" Seth asked, apparently so upset that he hadn't until that moment realized she was standing right there.

"Just visiting the rabbits."

"You should ask Silas about our trial drug your furry friends are involved in." Seth half-smiled. Glancing at his watch, he said, "Well, I shall leave you two alone. See you later."

When he was gone, Silas exhaled deeply and took a big gulp of coffee.

"Jessie, some of these rabbits have malignant tumors in their abdomen, kidneys and liver. The preclinical trial drug we are using will be closely monitored for safety, side effects, and effectiveness on the tumors. If we are successful, we'll step into the phase of using 10 to 20 humans in the study."

"That is so exciting."

"I also would like you to know that my friend Fawn, whom you met, has been diagnosed with malignant tumors in her kidneys and abdomen. Her treatment plan will be reviewed with her physician, Dr. Gunner, and her oncologist, Dr. de Lemon next week. She's really concerned about her child in the event of her death."

Jessica stood in silence feeling as though her heart was wedged in her throat like an oversized olive. "What an awful thing to happen to a young mother. I can't imagine leaving a young child behind." Smiling, then, to cover her discomfort, she said, "I must go now. Thanks for the information."

"Okay," Silas nodded.

When Jessica returned to the library, her thoughts were still about

Fawn. She hoped the drug would be successful.

It was difficult to concentrate, so she decided to look in on some of her post-surgical patients. Walking down the hallway, she saw at the far end Gunner talking to Antony, shouting and flinging his arms in the air. She couldn't quite hear what he was saying, but his gestures indicated he most definitely was not happy. She dodged into a room to her right, which luckily turned out to be occupied by one of her patients. She looked at the nurse's notes on the patient's chart attached at the foot of the bed. The patient was doing well, according to the nurse. Jessica did a quick physical exam and confirmed this. Then, she peeked out the door. Gunner was walking down the corridor toward her.

"Good day, Dr. Gunner," she said politely.

"Well, if it isn't the pony-tailed surgeon. I see you'll be graduating soon. Any future plans?" he asked, watching her closely. He was wearing his contact lenses, which tempted her to ask where his bifocals were.

"No plans yet."

"I spoke with a sister at the monastery, who indicated that you toured the children's care center—with Dr. Brown, no less. What did you think you were doing, touring a place like that?" he growled. "The sister also mentioned that you picked up your kid. Good God, you have a kid! And at that daycare center?"

"Yes. And Dr. Brown was just interested in seeing the facility. What's your point?"

"Look here, doctor," he said, irritated. "Let me remind you that I'm on the monastery board and have the authority to make life miserable for you." He was out of control. Jessica wondered if his attack on her had to do with either Finny being at the monastery or his argument with Antony. Gunner glared at her, turned on his heels with his face flaming red, and disappeared around the corner.

Jessica stood still for a moment with her hand clasped. Then, grinning wickedly, she muttered, "I got your meaning."

At the end of rounds, Jessica immediately went home and fortified herself with a large vodka and orange juice and retreated to her recliner. Would Gunner really make her life miserable? "Never," she promised herself. "Who does he think he is? God?" She was unsure whether the swell of raw emotion rising in her chest was anger or anguish. She retreated still further into the safety that being in her recliner always made her feel. When the phone rang, she let the answering machine pick up the call.

Later that evening, Cheyenne arrived home with Finny, who stretched out his arms and yelled, "Mama!" Jessica picked him up and showered him with kisses. She was filled with joy and love. He was evermore her shining star.

Cheyenne said she needed help with some questions about pathology, specifically about cellular division.

"Can we do it first thing in the morning?" Jessica replied. "I'm really exhausted." To which, Cheyenne replied, "Alright."

In the morning, the specter of Gunner seemed far away. Jessica and Cheyenne talked about pathology while they had breakfast, and Finny banged on his highchair and grinned while he was fed.

CHAPTER EIGHTEEN

A n ambulance screamed to a halt as it approached the Oregon Hospital and Science University Emergency Room accompanied by two police cars. Jessica looked out the hospital window and then heard the ER code announced over the intercom.

She had just finished operating on a major case with Dr. Stout. Still gowned, she walked into the ER and glanced about the room as residents and nurses swarmed in. Squeezing past the crowd on her way to the patient, Jessica bumped into a police officer who turned to her and said, "Excuse me, doctor, but I need to ask the injured man some questions."

The resident standing nearest the patient said, "This man is unconscious."

Jessica asked the officer, "What happened to him?"

"He was hit by a bus while crossing a major intersection against a green light."

"My God." Jessica approached the patient. His breath reeked of alcohol, and it was difficult to tell who he might be or even to recognize arms, legs and torso under all the blood. She could see blood running from the patient's hand and pumping from a punctured leg, soaking the sheets on the gurney.

"He must've received a laceration to the femoral artery," she said to Dr. Stout, who had not been quite as quick as she to reach the patient. Taking charge, she ordered: "Everyone leave, except fourth-year residents and ER nurses." Turning to the charge nurse, Jessica said, "Please call Dr. Brown immediately." Dr. Stout followed her lead, standing by her side.

The patient was put on a ventilator, an intravenous was started, and a series of X-rays were ordered of the abdomen, chest, and upper and lower extremities. Blood was drawn and sent to the laboratory to determine blood type and blood alcohol level. A urinary catheter inserted into his bladder instantly produced bloody urine. The patient was rushed to the Operating Room, Jessica and Dr. Stout following closely behind.

The radiologist read the X-rays and sent them to Max, who had already arrived in the OR. Max turned from the X-rays to Dr. Stout and Jessica and announced something almost unbelievable: "This is Dr. Gunner."

"He has a ruptured spleen," Max went on, "a collapsed lung, fractures to the arm and leg, and by the looks of the bloody urine, trauma to his lower abdomen."

Jessica looked at the man again. "He's still alive."

"He's a nasty, hateful man," Max said softly, "but we must do our jobs. No head injury. That's good. We should be able to save him."

The anesthetist interrupted. "Doctor, the patient's blood pressure is falling. Pulse is rapid and scarcely detectible. Let's keep him from going into shock."

"Nurse," Max yelled, "add a unit of blood to the intravenous. And inject epinephrine directly into the tubing to stimulate the heart."

Max, along with Dr. Stout and Jessica, performed a splenectomy, inserted a chest tube into the pleural cavity to help drain air and fluid, allowing the lung to re-expand, and then they repaired the femoral artery. His fractured arm and leg were set and casts applied.

Four hours later, just before Dr. Gunner was to be taken to the intensive care unit for post-surgery observation, Jessica stepped to the head of the gurney and pulled back his gown at the shoulder. And there it was, the subject of her nightmares: the tattoo of a bald eagle holding a double lightning rod. A thunderous wave of nausea punched her. "Excuse me, I'll be back in a minute," she said and dashed into the nearest restroom.

Gripping the edge of a toilet seat, Jessica vomited into the porcelain basin. She sat on the toilet then, feeling woozy, and within seconds vomited again. After that, she felt empty. She stepped to the sink, rinsed her mouth and glanced in the mirror. Her face had paled and her eyes looked glassy. It was as though she'd encountered the devil himself. After four years, she'd found him. "He's the bastard who raped me," she told her reflection. Then nausea struck again, and she wretched, but this time her stomach was empty.

She walked to the Intensive Care Unit and spotted Max at the nurses' station writing orders, instructing nursing staff to monitor the chest tube for air leaks, observe the patient for breathing difficulties, and carefully check for infection. Deep breathing and coughing was to be encouraged. These would help facilitate drainage and lung re-expansion.

When Max finished writing, he turned and noticed Jessica waiting for him. "Dr. Stout said he was exhausted and left for the day." Max said. "How about you and me have a cup of coffee and maybe a croissant? I'm sure we're both tired, too, and could use some sustenance." He frowned and looked at her more closely. "Are you okay?"

"Yes. Thanks for your concern. I'd like coffee." Jessica replied. Fatigue and tension were battling for control of her mind. She found herself almost thinking aloud, "Maybe Gunner won't survive."

In the coffee shop, they ordered and sat down with relief. Max lit a cigarette.

Jessica made eye contact, gently grasped Max's forearm, smiled, and said, "Max, I only have a few months until I graduate. Frankly, I can't wait to make up the time I missed during pregnancy."

"I'm still waiting to hear what your plans are after that."

Jessica so admired Max's patience and kindness that she almost said, right then and there, that her plans were to be with him. The only problem with that is she didn't know whether she wanted to be with him as business partner, as life partner, or maybe even both. So she just said, "I'll let you know soon. I promise."

Max cleared his throat and said, "Jessica, will you look in on Karl Gunner before you go home? I have a presentation to give, so I'll be leaving soon." He glanced at his watch. "If you have questions, page me."

Several hours later, Jessica walked into the Intensive Care Unit.

120

Her heart was pounding as she loomed over Dr. Gunner. If there was ever a time to get back at him for what he had done to her, it was now. She inhaled deeply, pulled a stethoscope from her coat pocket, placed it on his chest, and listened to his heart and lungs.

Gunner opened his eyes slowly, blinking. He was conscious but seemed dazed. He reached out and patted Jessica's hand. For more than a minute, he said nothing. Then, in a near whisper, he said, "Well done." The words seemed to come out of him almost by themselves. These were the words he always used in class when a student gave an accurate, confident response to his questions.

Jessica fought to keep her thoughts under control. She checked his abdominal surgical site, chest tube, and his arm and leg. His didn't have any more seepage or drainage from the femoral artery, but on further examination, the site near the hip revealed a massive scar that looked like a baseball diamond. Jessica applied pressure to the area, which caused him to wince and involuntarily jerk his leg. A memory surfaced: after the rape, he had limped away. She swallowed hard and wondered if the wound was the result of his time in Vietnam during the war.

When she finished the exam, she said, "I'll see you tomorrow." She left hurriedly. At the nurses' station, she reread his chart and briefly discussed his care with the nurse in charge.

That evening at home, Cheyenne asked, "What really happened to Dr. Gunner? All the students were talking about his accident and injuries."

"Well, you'll no doubt hear all kinds of stories. The bottom line is he was drunk, crossed a busy intersection against a green light, and as a consequence got hit by a bus."

"Will he live?"

"I guess so." She stopped herself from saying, "I hope not."

Midmorning the next day, Jessica entered the Intensive Care Unit and asked the nurse in charge how Dr. Gunner's night had gone. Uneventful, she was told. She entered his room, stood at the foot of his bed and said, "How is Dr. Gunner this morning?" Her voice was icy and her eyes deadly. At that moment, the door opened, and Max entered. "Good morning, Jessica." Max smiled at her before turning to Dr. Gunner. "Karl, how are you feeling?"

"Every damn muscle and bone in my body hurts."

"Well, you're lucky you didn't break your neck. We'll get the pain under control, but now I'd like to examine you."

"The pony-tailed doctor examined me earlier." The nurse standing by the bedside gasped at Dr. Gunner's remark.

Max glared at him. "Karl, that is inappropriate. This doctor's name is Dr. Tinker." He pointed at Jessica. "And by the way, Karl, if it hadn't been for Dr. Tinker, you might not even be alive. She was the first on the scene and made all the right calls.

Dr. Gunner apparently embarrassed, said, "All right, all right. I've been pumped full of medications, so my thinking is probably a bit fuzzy."

The nurse looked horrified.

Max performed the exam and looked at the scar that Jessica had noted earlier. "Karl, how did you get this scar?"

"During my tour of duty in Nam. One night, one of the members of our patrol unit stepped on a landmine. The explosion killed him instantly. I was far enough away to miss death, but I was wounded and airlifted to Hanoi. Doctors removed the shrapnel, and then I was flown to the States."

"I understand." Max said.

Later, in the doctors' lounge, Jessica and Max discussed Gunner's future hospital care and his follow-up care in physical therapy. Max told Jessica that the hospital's CEO had asked him to fill in for Dr. Gunner while he was recovering.

"Oh," she said. "Are you going to?"

"I'm not sure. I'd like your input."

"Gee, Max, does that mean you won't be setting up a private practice?"

"Well, he responded. It seems there is no one else to fill Gunner's position. If I do take this on, it might be four months at most."

"Take it," she decided. "I'll have graduated by that time. I was planning to visit my mother in Seattle and ask for financial help for the construction of your surgical clinic. That is, if we become equal partners." She shifted nervously. "Would you consider driving with me to Seattle to talk to her?"

He smiled widely. "Not only would I consider driving with you, but I'm ecstatic that you're joining me at my—I mean, our—future surgery clinic. When do you plan on leaving for Seattle?"

"In a couple of weeks or so."

"Good."

"Max, before you go, I'd like to tell you what happened to me in the OR." She almost started to cry.

"What is it, Jessica?" Max put his arm around her shoulder.

"When I ran out just before Gunner was wheeled into the ICU Recovery Room," she gasped. "It was because..."

Max interrupted. "You pulled the hospital gown off Dr. Gunner's shoulder. What were you looking for?"

"He.... He...." She sniffled. "Four years ago, Gunner raped me. It happened after one of the Snow's parties. I was walking to my car late that evening when he attacked me. I ripped his shirt and saw the tattoo—the same one I saw when I pulled off his hospital gown."

"Dear Lord! Did you go to the police?"

"No. I was worried about publicity, and I was so ashamed that I had let something like that happen to me. And I didn't know who he was—at the time."

She might have said more, but just then two doctors walked into the lounge and sat nearby. So both she and Max stood and left.

Two week passed. Each time Jessica saw Max, he would reach out and touch her gently on the shoulder, telling her without words that while he couldn't understand what she felt, he could, and did, feel for her. Meanwhile, Dr. Gunner's recovery progressed favorably. His chest tube was removed and he was transferred to a private room on the surgical floor.

As usual one mid-morning, Jessica approached the nurses' station and asked how Dr. Gunner's night had been, checked notes written overnight, and entered his room to examine him. She had made up her mind: that day, she would tell him she knew he was her rapist.

He was lying in bed quietly, eyes closed, and a recorder was playing music by Schumann. He looked up, half-smiling, and turned the recorder off. Standing next to his bed and satisfied that no one was nearby, Jessica said, "You will pay for what you did to me over four years ago. You will feel the pain I felt!" Her stomach muscles tightened as she struggled to hold back the urge to suffocate him with the very pillow on which he lay.

He said nothing. Perhaps he wasn't sure whether to counter attack or admit his wrongdoing. His chin quivered as he said, "What are you talking about?"

Jessica looked down into the cruel face of her attacker and said, "You rapist, you know damn well what I'm talking about."

"You better be damn sure you have your facts in order. You can't prove anything. For that matter, no one will believe you. I've been here for years. I'm the chairman of the hospital board. I'm a top-notch surgeon. So, what are you going to do about it? The statute of limitations has expired. And I can ruin your career."

He didn't even deny raping her. "I'm going to hang you out to dry, rapist! What you've done to me is despicable. I'll find a way to get you. I'll see you sent to prison for the rest of your rotten life. You're nothing more than a drunk criminal with a filthy mouth."

"And you're a goody-goody who had a kid." He wiped his nose with the back of his hand and swallowed hard. "How old is the kid?"

"Why? Are you concerned he might be yours? Don't worry your smutty mind. I would rather die and burn in hell than carry your child."

She placed her hand into her white coat jacket, pulled out a small booklet the size of an address book, and threw it on his chest. "Read this a thousand times and ask the Lord to cleanse your soul."

He glanced at the booklet and said, "A Bible?" He had a wide grin on his aging face.

Jessica took a deep breath and continued. "Furthermore, if you ever refer to me as the pony-tailed doctor again, I will kill you. You'll never know or suspect when it will happen, and I'll skin that bald eagle tattoo right off your arm." Her eyes wild, she turned and stormed out of the room, beads of sweat covering her forehead.

Later that morning, Max, not knowing that Jessica had confronted Dr. Gunner earlier about the rape, examined the man and then asked, "Karl, how long have you known Dr. Tinker? He eyed Gunner, watching for a change in expression.

Gunner's cheeks and neck became slightly flushed. "Why do you ask?"

"I have my reasons."

"What the hell does that mean?" Angry, he shifted in bed, trying to sit up.

There was something animal-like about him, something demanding and harsh, Max thought. But as disturbing as that aspect of him was, Max had to admit the man seemed confident when he replied, "I don't know for certain. About four years or so. Let's see, yes, she's been here four years."

"Did you know her before that?"

"Of course not." Dr. Gunner's gaze wandered fiercely around the room.

Max didn't pursue the issue. He rubbed the back of his neck and wondered if he should tell Karl that the hospital board had asked him to serve during his absence. Deciding against it, he said, "Karl, I have a lot to do. See you later," He turned and left.

CHAPTER NINETEEN

The temperature had dropped drastically. Standing outside the hospital after work, Jessica buttoned her windbreaker and turned to face the freezing winds gusting from the Columbia Gorge and whipping through her hair. It was invigorating.

Walking to her car, she thought it would be wise to call her mother and thank her again for everything she'd done to help her throughout her schooling. However, Max had told her that her mother had called him with prying questions, and Jessica was cautious now about having any conversation with her mother until she found out why her mother would try to meddle in Max's private life.

No way to solve that problem at the moment. Were there any problems she could solve? Well, maybe a check on how Dr. Gunner was doing would be good. She retraced her steps back into the hospital just in time to see Max walking into Gunner's room, leaving the door ajar. She peeked around the door.

"How are you feeling?" asked Max.

"Fine, just fine," replied Gunner.

"Let's examine you and see if you're ready for discharge."

"I am sure as hell ready to resume my duties." he sounded both desperate and angry. "And return to my position as chairman of the board. You can resign now, Max."

Max reached out and put his arm on Karl's shoulder. He said firmly, "I don't think it's advisable for you to take on too much responsibility all at once. I recommend you start by seeing a few patients. Perhaps later, you can return to your board position."

"To hell with that! Are you trying to monopolize my position?" Now, Gunner's voice was definitely angry. Jessica hoped Max wouldn't cave in and let Gunner go back to running the show.

"No, Karl. For medical reasons, I'm recommending that you be fully-recovered before returning to your responsibilities. You need to continue with physical therapy, and I'll see you in my office in two weeks. In one week, you need to see your orthopedic doctor for cast removal. Do you have any questions?" Max remained professional, but his voice penetrated.

Dr. Gunner responded with the respect a tyrant sometimes gives to someone he deems competent. "I'll see you in two weeks. And I'll get the cast removed in a week."

Max turned to walk out of the room, and Jessica dashed back to the nurses' desk. She smiled and said, "Hi, Max."

"What are you doing here?" he asked. He wasn't smiling. Maybe he was recovering from the negative encounter with Gunner.

"I'm just about to visit Silas's friend, Fawn," she said. "She was admitted several days ago. Would you like to come with me to see her?"

"Sure, but I can only stay a few minutes."

"Thanks, I appreciate it. Did you discharge Gunner?" she asked.

"Yes. He thinks he's ready to return to work at full speed, but he's sicker than he thinks. He still has a cast on his arm and leg, and he needs long-term physical therapy. His face and body remain bruised, and his ribs need healing." Max stopped for a moment and said, "He's such an obstinate man."

Jessica added, "He thinks he's God—powerful and mighty." She paused. "I wish he had died in that accident." Then she felt embarrassed about expressing her feelings and lowered her head in shame.

Max's reply was consoling: "It's okay. I understand why."

The two of them walked to Fawn's room, and when they arrived, Silas was already there. He stood as Max and Jessica walked in.

"Hello, Fawn, Silas. How do you feel today, Fawn?" Jessica asked.

"Silas tells me the word is stable," Fawn said. "I'm still experiencing nausea, though, and I still throw up sometimes." She looked over at Silas and smiled.

Jessica turned her head in disbelief as Gunner walked in wearing his white coat. He pulled a stethoscope from his coat pocket while using crutches to maintain balance. "Well, well, if it isn't the medical clan. I ask that everyone leave. I prefer a one-on-one exam with my patient. I don't need a nurse, or any doctors." He glanced at Jessica.

Max wrinkled his brow and whispered to Jessica, "He was just discharged. What in God's name is wrong with him? I should have referred him for psychiatric therapy. Let's go. I'll buy you a cup of coffee."

The three doctors said goodbye to Fawn, left the room and headed for the coffee shop. They sat at a corner table. Jessica gulped her cup of coffee and went for a refill.

When she returned, Silas and Max were talking about Fawn.

"It doesn't sound very hopeful," Max was saying.

"What do you mean?" Jessica asked as she sat down.

Silas said, "Fawn has lost weight, has no appetite, and remains nauseated and weak. There doesn't seem much hope for her survival unless the chemotherapy works."

They spent a short time discussing Fawn's condition before parting company. "I'll come by in a few minutes to see the rabbits, just as soon as I've had a chance to talk with Fawn," Jessica told Silas as he headed back to the lab. She stood, squeezed Max's shoulders and kissed his cheek, and left.

Entering Fawn's room, she saw that the nurse was giving her a back rub. "Dr. Tinker," the nurse said. "I'll be finished in a moment."

"No rush." Jessica pulled up a chair and sat.

"You look nice," Fawn said, glancing over at her. "Today, my sister, Ann Lake, is bringing my son to visit. I'm excited to see him.""

"That's good news. It's good of your sister to bring him.

Just then, much to Jessica's disappointment, Gunner entered the room again. Jessica scooted her chair away from the bed but remained seated. Gunner turned to her and said, "This will take a while. We need to discuss medical issues and care."

She remained seated and replied, "That sounds good."

Face flushed, Gunner said, "Don't you have patients to see?"

"I made my rounds earlier."

"Look, young lady, I want you to leave. Now!"

Jessica stood, squeezed Fawn's hand, and said, "I'll see you later," and left the room.

She went to check on the progress of the rabbits. She was still waiting for Silas in the lab when suddenly Gunner came in shouting, "Seth, its Karl. Do you have a minute to talk?" She moved out of sight, not wanting to get in the man's way again.

Seth appeared and said, "Talk? Talk about what?"

"Nothing specific. How are things going with your research?"

"Just great."

"I want you to know that I'm recovering nicely and find physical therapy helpful. I will be returning as chairman of the board just as soon as I feel normal. That will be a few weeks from now, perhaps even days."

Silas appeared from behind the desk and, seeing Gunner but not Seth, asked, "Can we be of any help?" Jessica knew him well enough to know he was irritated.

"No, no, no. I'm fine. Dr. Gunner paused, shifted his weight onto his uninjured leg, and said, "How's your trial drug study coming along with the rabbits?"

He addressed Silas, but Seth replied. "Ten to 20 percent of the tumors are in various stages of resolution. The treated rabbits have had minimal loss of appetite, though some have been sluggish. Otherwise, no major side effects. So far they are tolerating the drug."

"I'd like to take a peek at the rabbits, just to see how they look."

"By all means, go ahead and look," Seth said.

Gunner's eyes locked in on Silas as he walked past Seth's desk and into the room where the rabbits were kept. He still had not seen Jessica. She had told Silas that Gunner always seemed to compete for power, money, and recognition, and he had admitted he disliked the man intensely. He had even said he hoped the hospital board would dismiss him as chief of surgery and hospital chairman. Both he and Jessica thought Seth was being very tolerant of his frequent drop-ins, his curiosity, and his eagerness to get information about the latest experimental drug study.

Seth now was saying, "Silas, why don't you take your break, and I'll join you promptly in the coffee shop? Karl, when you're finished studying the rabbits, let the secretary know when you leave. I plan to join Silas on a break."

"Good," said Gunner. "Don't worry. I'll close the door quietly." Did the man always have to sound so sarcastic and cynical?

CHAPTER TWENTY

J essica arrived home from an evening medical meeting. When she walked in the apartment, Cheyenne announced, "Finny's been fed, dressed for bed, and is now playing with his toys in the living room."

Jessica said "Thank you" and meant it. She was tired and achy after a very long day. She dashed into the living room, picked Finny up, and flooded him with kisses and hugs. Cheyenne had a date for the evening and left shortly after that, while Jessica tucked him into bed.

With Finny's giggles no longer heard, Jessica thought her apartment seemed... empty, like an echo in an empty space. She thought about how hollow her life would be without Finny. She'd always seen herself as an outsider, always been a little lonely, but now she had someone to love.

She made herself a large mug of Lipton tea and relaxed in her recliner for a few minutes. Then, she phoned her mother and thanked her once again for all the financial help she'd received from her.

She intended to ask her mother about a loan to start the clinic, but something—it was hard to put a finger on what, exactly—held her back. Maybe it was that phone call her mother had made to Max.

Max, she thought, *is truly a good friend.* He's never deceptive, and he always analyzes both sides of an issue before expressing an idea or opinion. Silas, on the other hand, seems to be more secretive, not always so forthcoming. And Jessica had to admit she was still puzzled by his undefined relationship with Fawn.

After finishing her tea, she walked into the kitchen and looked for something to eat. Then on the spur of the moment, she changed her mind, picked up the phone, and began to dial Max's number. Then, uncertain about whether he would think she was pursuing, and even more uncertain about whether that would be okay, she placed the receiver in its cradle and went to bed.

In the morning, Jessica scurried out of bed and looked out the window at what was shaping up to be a beautiful September day. She stood up as straight as she could, squared her shoulders, and then put her hands on her lower back. Bending backward, she tried to stretch muscles that had become sore from long hours of standing and stooping over surgery cases. Once she graduated, she'd be in a position to set her own schedule. Surely then, her back would not be this painful.

Jessica would be graduating soon. She planned to continue working at the hospital, at least for a while. She was both excited and unsure about her future, but she still held out hope that her mother would lend her the money for the private clinic that was to begin construction within a month. Her choice to partner with Max felt like a wise decision.

After breakfast, she showered, dressed herself and Finny, put the dishes into the dishwasher, and took Finny to the monastery. As she was leaving the care center, she saw Gunner walking with one of the sisters down the long hallway. She left quickly using the side door and rushed to her car. She got in, inhaled deeply, and tried to calm down. Her heart continued to pound. She needed to take control of herself. She couldn't let just seeing this evil turn her into a frightened little girl.

She sat in her car for almost 20 minutes, and at that point spotted Gunner leaving the monastery and heading for his car. He glanced at his watch, swung his arm in frustration as if whipping a horse, and got into his car. But he didn't start the engine. Jessica wondered why and decided to wait and see. Ten minutes later, who should show up but Antony Scolari.

Antony parked parallel to Gunner and then joined him in his car. They were together almost 15 minutes talking to each other. Jessica had now seen them in intimate conversation a number of times. She was becoming convinced there was some conspiracy between these two men, particularly since by now, all hospital construction and renovation was complete. She decided to try and keep an eye on both of them.

She drove to the hospital, parked, and entered the library. Her pager buzzed. Realizing it was Max, she stepped into the hallway to speak with him.

"What's up?" she asked.

"I'd like you to set aside next Friday evening." He paused for a moment. "I'd like to take you to the Benson Hotel to celebrate your graduation." I called your mother—yes, your mother—and she wants to come, too."

"But I..."

"Listen, Jessica, graduation is a once-in-a-lifetime event. I'm planning on inviting some of your friends, too, for a big dinner party. Is there anyone you don't want me to invite?"

Without hesitation, she said, "Absolutely not Gunner."

"Of course, not him. I wouldn't invite him," replied Max.

"Why are you doing this, Max?"

"Because you mean a lot to me, Jessica. I care a great deal about you. Now, I'll pick you up at five on Friday."

"Can you come a little sooner and help me get Finny ready?"

There was a silence, and then Max said, "You want to bring him to this celebration? He's not quite a year and a half. This is a party: eating, drinking, dancing, and lots of noise."

Jessica considered this and said, "Yes, Max, you're right. He is too young for these things. But come over earlier anyway, okay?" She realized she felt relieved to not have to bring Finny. Then she felt guilty. *Don't I spend enough time with him?*, she thought. *Well, of course I do.*

She wondered what to wear to the party. Her closet held a few items she could mix and match for evening wear, but she knew that this would be a night to remember. She wanted to look attractive and intelligent to impress her mother and, of course, Max. She stayed in the library most of the day catching up on all her medical logs and required reading—business before pleasure—but come late afternoon, she went shopping.

Early Friday evening, the doorbell rang. The door swung open, and Jessica, still dressed casually, said, "Come in. Thanks for coming early."

Max handed her a bouquet of red carnations. "Congratulations," he said smiling. He was dressed for the occasion in a white shirt, maroon tie, and navy suit.

"Wow. These are breathtaking, and they smell so sweet." Please make yourself a drink while I shower and dress. The babysitter should be here soon. Cheyenne is out for the evening. Thanks again for hosting my graduation dinner party, Max. And, hey, you look smashing."

Max smiled even wider. "Thank you for the complement." His eyes were full of laughter, but his voice was solemn.

"I'll get some wine," he said, and stepped into the kitchen for the bottle and two stemmed glasses.

As he poured, he said, "I'm proud of your success." They raised their glasses simultaneously. "Cheers."

"I'll be back in a jiffy. Please watch Finny," Jessica said, disappearing into the bedroom. Twenty minutes later, she emerged and posed for him like a model.

Max looked at her and said, "You're so slim and beautiful, and your hair is so shiny."

She had bought a black, long-sleeved, flowing dress with a deep v-neckline. It was mid-length with an inset pocket on the hip that emphasized what she thought to be her best feature: a small waist. She was ready to dance the night away.

"I sure hope Mother comes up with the loan, Max," she said. "Did she mention anything about it when you called her about the party?"

"No, not that I recall." He said, "Excuse me. I left something in my car." He left and then returned right away with a box wrapped in shiny white paper and tied with black ribbons attached to a large black bow.

"The wrapping paper is beautiful," she said.

"Open it," Max said.

She pulled on the ribbons and ran a finger under the package sides to release the tape. Unwrapping the box and unfolding the pink paper inside, she pulled out a pair of fur slippers.

"Oh, my goodness! I don't know what to say. These are beautiful." She stepped out of her pumps and slipped her feet into the soft fur. She looked up at Max and gave him a hug and a kiss. "I feel like Cinderella."

Max smiled at the admiration in her eyes.

The baby sitter arrived, and Jessica gave her instructions about Finny's care and wrote down both her and Max's pager numbers, in the event of an emergency. Then, she and Max left for the party.

In the car, Max pressed her about her plans for the future. She reiterated that her near-term plans were to become his partner in a clinic she would help him build with her mother's money, that is, if Mother would loan her some. "But long term," she admitted, "I want to become a neurosurgeon."

"You have high ambitions. What about marriage? A family, a home?"

"I don't know." A memory flashed by--Silas turning his back on her.

When they pulled up in front of the Benson Hotel, Jessica was so anxious to avoid the whole marriage-and-family thing that she started to climb out of the car without waiting for Max to open her door. He pulled her back in.

"Don't get out yet," he said.

So, it was a few more moments of talk about Max's mother and father and their 40-year marriage, and how much he wanted a wife, and didn't she want a husband? She murmured "Hmm" and "Oh, yes," but the memory and pain of Silas leaving was still strong.

Ten minutes later, they walked into the Benson Hotel and into Trader Vic's Restaurant. Everyone stood and shouted, "Congratulations, Jessica." She looked around at the crowd, and there were her friends all happy and clapping in a room festooned with balloons, streamers, and swags. The tables each held a bouquet of pink roses. She spotted a middle-aged lady sitting in the corner with a big purse, her hair curled. She was wearing heavy makeup and clapping like everyone else.

"Thank you, thank you, everyone. She smiled from ear to ear, and then added, "Special thanks to Dr. Max Brown for arranging this whole event. This is indeed a day I will remember."

She suddenly realized the lady in the corner was her mother. Her mother never wore her hair in tight curls, and even more of a surprise, she never sat quietly. Could a group of doctor scholars have intimidated her?

Everyone crowded around, and Jessica found herself getting and giving lots of hugs. When Silas appeared in front of her, she was taken aback for a moment, not expecting him to be here. "Hello, Silas," she said in an impartial tone.

"Jessie, you look beautiful."

She hugged him then, and said, "I'm glad you were able to come." It was a lie. She wanted to hurt him, to have him see her with Max, but at the same time she wanted to share her joy at graduation with him, as her friend. "How's Fawn?"

"She's still in the hospital." He winced. "She's not doing well."

"I'll spend some time with her tomorrow. It's my day off."

"I think she'd like that."

Jessica moved on and chatted briefly with Leslie and Alexander, Dr. Stout and his wife, and Seth, who said only that the rabbits were doing well.

Cheyenne stepped into her circle of friends to introduce her parents. "Cheyenne! I really thought you were going on a date tonight.

You fooled me." They both laughed.

Max stepped next to Jessica, put his arm around her waist, and announced that dinner was about to be served. Everyone was seated while a rock band played. Jessica's mother sat next to her daughter.

"Jessica, your stepfather wasn't well enough to travel, but he sends his best."

After the main course—baked ham with a plum-and-mustard glaze served with asparagus and new potatoes—Max asked Jessica to dance, and soon Cheyenne's parents and Dr. Stout and his wife joined them. Seth and Silas sat at the table and chatted, but Silas kept glancing at Jessica. It seemed he *was* noticing her with Max. *Good.* Jessica thought.

"Oh," said Max in mid-waltz. "It almost slipped my mind. The Mother Superior replied to my invitation to this party. She mailed you a congratulatory card to my office address because she couldn't find yours. No one from the monastery could attend your party, of course, but she conveyed their best wishes."

"That was considerate of them," Jessica said.

When chocolate trifle was served, everyone sat except Silas, who'd asked Cheyenne to dance. He held her close but continued to keep an eye on his *Jessie*, occasionally glaring at Max. At the end of the dance, he left the room.

The next morning, Jessica got out of bed and went to the window. A late-autumn sky seemed to be draped warmly over the tree tops. Despite a headache, she said to herself, "This is the beginning of a beautiful day." While showering, she reviewed the previous evening, impressed with how well Max had organized her dinner party. She told herself he'd be an excellent business partner. But for that to happen, she had to come up with her share of the startup costs. Her mother hadn't even hinted about helping her. She hadn't even given her a graduation gift. "Well," she said aloud, "It is a beautiful day and I'll have to think about getting financial help some other way."

She dressed in jeans and a navy polo shirt, and did her hair up in her usual ponytail, and then got Finny up and dressed. They were in the kitchen getting a breakfast together when she heard a knock on the door. She opened it, and there stood Max and her mother. She invited them in for coffee.

At the kitchen table, her mother opened her big purse, pulled out a small, simply-wrapped package, handed it to Jessica, and said, "Congratulations, honey. I'm very proud of you."

"Thank you, Mother." She felt a wave of warmth sweep over her.

Max sipped his coffee and smiled. "Open it," he said. Turning to Finny, who was on his lap, he said, "Don't you think Mama should open the package?"

Finny shook his head yes, and then said, "Papa." It was a word he had probably learned at the daycare. Recently, Finny's language development had taken off like a rocket. Max seemed to be enjoying the ride.

Jessica opened the box and went pale, speechless, looking at a check inside the box for $100,000. "Max, look at this." she said, handing him the check. "Oh, Mother, thank you!" She hugged her mother tight. "This will pay for more than half of my share!" She rushed over to Finny and kissed him, and then she kissed Max, too, fervently. By now, she was crying. Then she looked Max in the eye. "Max, did you and Mother cook this surprise up?"

"Your mother and I have struggled to keep this a secret for some time."

Jessica laughed, plucked a tissue from her pocket and dabbed at her eyes. "Mother, I'm so grateful for your help. Always. I didn't realize you could keep such a great secret."

"You're my only child," her mother said reasonably. "I'm happy to be able to help."

"Mother, you and Max planned this party well. You had me snowed completely. Thank you again, and I love you both." She realized she had included Max when she'd said, "love." She had finally told him the truth.

"Well, folks." Max said. "Are we ready for a hearty breakfast?"

They agreed they were and left for the restaurant.

On the drive there, Max said, "Jessica, some time ago, when land was less expensive, I bought a small parcel of land downtown overlooking the Willamette River. We can build our clinic there. The land will be my single contribution."

Jessica carefully matched his beaming expression and tone of voice as she responded, "Sounds great. My single contribution will be to purchase some of the surgical equipment."

Her mother said nothing, while maintaining a pleasant smile.

"What do you think, Mother?" Jessica asked, turning her head toward the back seat.

"Well, she said, grinning, "I hope to get a permanent free pass to your clinic when it's constructed." That got the three of them laughing.

CHAPTER TWENTY-ONE

It was seven in the morning when Dr. Gunner entered Fawn's hospital room with a smile and said, "Good morning." His voice was cheerful. "Fawn, what sort of night did you have?" He wore a wrinkled white coat, his face was unshaven, and his nose and cheeks appeared more ruddy than usual.

"I had a horrible night. I couldn't sleep. The nausea was very intense. I vomited."

"I'll order medication to be injected into your intravenous, which should help with the nausea. I'll examine you now and return later to check on you again after the anti-nausea medication takes effect." He examined her, added his notes to her chart. Then he went and bought a dozen doughnuts at the coffee shop and headed for the research lab.

When he entered, Silas immediately asked, "How is Fawn this morning?"

"I prescribed Phenergan for her nausea. It should make her feel better. The oncologist will be seeing her later this morning." He paused. "Is Seth in?"

"Yes. Just wait here. I'll get him."

When Seth appeared, Gunner handed him the box of doughnuts. "What's this, some sort of bribery?" Seth frowned. "How can I help you?"

"Just wanted to tell you that I've returned to serve as chairman of the board. My injuries are healing well, and there's less pain in the fractured leg, the one I injured while in Vietnam. Physical therapy is helping greatly."

Seth nodded, his frown gone. Gunner was a patient, so he should be treated with respect. "Karl," Seth said, "the rabbits are recovering at an incredible rate without detrimental side effects. If this continues, we'll soon be able to start our first human trial of the drug."

Gunner looked at Silas and said, "If all this works, it might save many lives someday. Too bad it can't help Fawn because it's still in preclinical trials." There was no regret in his voice.

There was again some animosity in Silas's response. "With your knowledge and expertise in patient management, there's no reason why she shouldn't improve. Is there?"

There was silence for a moment. Then Gunner said to Seth, "Enjoy the goodies," and left.

He returned less than a week later in a rush, almost mowing down the lab's secretary on her way out. "Sorry, Seth," he gasped, trying to get his breath back. "I ran here all the way from Fawn's room."

"In God's name, man! What happened?" Seth pulled out a chair from behind a desk and said, "Here, Karl, sit down."

Gunner was like a child who's just been given a lollipop. "It's a miracle, Seth. Fawn's health had been failing at an incredible rate, and my plan was to recommend hospice care. But this morning, she sat up in bed with a big grin and said some of her nausea and weakness had subsided and that she'd even had a protein bar for breakfast." He paused, looked around and said, "Is Silas off today?"

"Yes, he really deserves a rest. He's been so devoted to our trial research project."

"I see. That reminds me about Fawn's general depression. Silas visits her very frequently. Several times a day, as a matter of fact, and with each visit, she gets more depressed after he leaves. He seems to have difficulty dealing with her cancer."

"Well, whether that's true or not, Karl, I know that Silas is not intending to upset Fawn or make her depressed. Maybe he had difficulty dealing with suffering and dying patients, I don't know. But I understand his concern and his wish to be available when Fawn needs him."

Gunner looked down at the floor, as though in search of something, and then muttered, "Don't mention this to Silas. No reason to stir up bad feelings." He looked at his watch, stood and said, "Thanks for listening." Getting up, he exited quickly.

Seth went to the rabbit cages and watched his experimental subjects play and eat. The rabbits seemed happy and healthy. He hoped they would continue to stay tumor-free. *Time to go home.* When he picked up his jacket and walked toward the door, however, he saw Jessica leaning against it.

"What are you doing here this late?" Seth said.

"Silas didn't answer his phone or pager, so I figured he might be here. I need to speak with him." Jessica replied.

"What's this all about? First Karl, and now you."

"I just visited Fawn. I'm amazed at her phenomenal improvement. She even mentioned going home, possibly tomorrow." Jessica was frowning.

"Well, that's thanks to the chemotherapy," Seth replied. "There are drugs that do work in certain cancers. We doctors don't always know a patient's outcome with certainty."

"Yes, I know, and I'm pleased she's better. I'm sorry for bothering you, but thanks for lending your ear." She smiled and said, "Goodnight."

"Goodnight," Seth replied, deciding after both Karl's and Jessica's visits that he would drop by and visit Fawn also, observe her improvement himself. When he entered Fawn's room, she and her oncologist looked up and stopped their spirited conversation. Fawn was bright-eyed. Her color had returned. She looked healthy.

Seth wished Fawn the best in recovery and left, the oncologist followed him. "I'm amazed to see such an improvement in Fawn."

The oncologist replied, "Well, I'm not surprised. We always try to use the appropriate chemotherapy for a particular cancer, and in many of our patients we see improvement and, sometimes, full resolution." The man was avoiding eye contact, shifting his weight from side to side, and glancing about as if speaking to an audience.

"Well, whatever the reason," Seth said, "I'm pleased she's better." And with that, he walked away.

CHAPTER TWENTY-TWO

Fawn was discharged the next week. Two weeks after that, Seth and Silas walked into the research lab in the morning to check on the rabbits and were horrified to see some of them curled up in the corner of their cage, inactive and listless, their food untouched. Seth paced for a few minutes, his shoulders stooped and face drawn, and said, "Silas, call the chemistry lab and have blood drawn on all the rabbits in the study immediately." He picked up one of the rabbits and discovered it was already dead. Both of them then quickly checked the others—half of those who were inactive in the corners of the cage were dead.

"Oh, my God," Seth exclaimed. "So much for our promising trial drug."

Just then, the phone rang, and Seth answered. It was a nurse who said, "Dr. Diesel, please inform Dr. Rolland that Fawn Juzel was readmitted very early this morning." She paused. "Her family has already been notified."

Seth thanked the nurse, sat down momentarily, shook his head, stood and stepped toward Silas. "You had best check on Fawn," he said. "She was readmitted very early this morning."

Silas paled and stared at Seth. "Thanks. You'll need to make the call to the lab for blood draws, then." He turned on his heel and almost flew to Fawn, checking her chart at the nurses' station and barreling into her room--to find Dr. Gunner already there, leaning over her with his stethoscope on her chest.

Gunner looked up at Silas and then at the nurse accompanying him. "She's gone," he said. Leaving the room, he bumped into Silas, who had come to a halt near the bed. A muscle in Silas's jaw twitched. Gunner said nothing to him; only shook his head, his demeanor flat as he walked to the nurses' desk, wrote a note in Fawn's chart and left. The nurse moved forward and pulled the curtain around Fawn's bed.

Silas pulled up a chair, sat at Fawn's bedside and gazed at her. He took her hand in his and stroked it gently, murmuring, "I'll miss you Fawn. You're a good person, a good friend. I-I wish I could've done more to help you." His eyes were wet with tears.

Suddenly, he stood, walked to the nurses' desk and asked for Fawn's chart. He read and reread every word that Gunner had written, his expression becoming more and more puzzled. He spotted a notation in Gunner's hand. In the margin, in very tiny print, he read "AVD 7008." That was the clinical name of experimental drug he and Seth had administered to the rabbits.

Silas thought it would be wise to have copies made of Fawn's lab reports and medical notes. He asked a nurse to print a copy of each. She did and handed them to him.

It was nighttime when Silas left the hospital after a horrific day tending to mostly dead rabbits and trying not to think about Fawn. Wearily, he got in his car, and drove home. When he stepped out of the car, he looked at the sky in wonder. He searched for constellations in the dark heavens and wondered if Fawn's spirit was somewhere out there, among the stars.

Quite late that night, Jessica received a call from him. She had already been informed of Fawn's death, so she was prepared to be consoling. Silas seemed not to need consolation so much as confirmation from her that she and Max would meet him Friday morning to go over Fawn's chart. He told her he had made a copy. She was curious, but she was also busy, so didn't think too much of it.

Friday morning, the trio met in the coffee shop and each ordered coffee. When it came, he took a sip, frowned, shook his head, and pulled copies of Fawn's chart with the lab findings and notes out of his briefcase. He gave Jessica and Max each a reprint and flipped through the pages of his own copy. "Ah, here it is," he said, his voice harsh, and directed them to the page where *AVD 7008* was written.

Max read Gunner's notation and said, "I'm totally at a loss as to why that drug name is written here, or for that matter anywhere in the chart."

"Let me take a closer look," Jessica said. With her elbows on the table and her hands supporting her head, she read everything word-for-word, occasionally looking up and making irritated 'hmm' and 'huh' sounds. "I don't trust Gunner," she concluded when she'd finished. She surveyed Max and Silas for any negative reactions to this statement, got none, and said firmly, "Silas, I think you need to consult an attorney. Call Alexander. He's smart, meticulous, and extremely capable."

Silas agreed, and the three of them made plans to attend Fawn's funeral service the next morning. Silas said that Fawn's sister, Ann Lake, had arranged the service, and the burial on the third day after her death. "At the request of her family, there was to be no autopsy," he said. Fawn had also not wanted an autopsy done if and when she died, since the cancer had invaded her body, and no studies would be of help.

Just then Silas's pager beeped. It was Seth, saying he should come to the research lab at once.

He excused himself from the group and headed to the lab. When Silas got there, he could tell that Seth had been pacing around his desk for a while.

He stopped inches from Silas's face and said, "You need to tell me about your relationship with Fawn."

"What do you mean? We were friends, nothing more."

"Did you think she was suffering too much, too long?"

"Why are you asking me these questions?"

"Well, first thing this morning when I arrived, Karl Gunner was waiting to speak with me about Fawn. He implied you might be involved in her sudden death in some way. He mentioned that you precipitated her depression."

"Involved? That's insane. Nuts. Gunner's a sick man."

"That's possible. But what worries me is that Fawn's symptoms and death followed a pattern identical to that of the rabbits."

"My God," Silas exclaimed. "Is it possible Gunner gave her the trial drug, thinking she'd recover like the rabbits did initially?"

Seth started to pace again. "I don't know."

"Seth, I want you to know that I reviewed Fawn's chart right after her death. I noticed a notation in the margin of the notes that looked as though it was written by Dr. Gunner. It was the name of our trial drug. How would he know the name? I never told him."

"I didn't either, but he may have seen the vials during one of his visits here. Silas, I've worked with you a long time, and I believe you to be a trustworthy research analyst."

"I am trustworthy."

"I know, I know. But has it occurred to you that you may have set yourself up to be blamed for Fawn's death?"

"How? Do you think Karl's trying to implicate me?" Suddenly, he could see it: He was her close friend. He visited her several times a day in the hospital and several times after she was released. He was working in research. He had access to the drug. Gunner could point the finger at him. No wonder Jessica had wanted him to see Alexander. "I'll need to consult an attorney about this," he announced.

"That is a good idea," Seth said.

Silas phoned the Snow Law Firm immediately.

CHAPTER TWENTY-THREE

S ilas arrived at the law office of Alexander Snow at precisely 10:15 a.m. to discuss Fawn's death and the possibility that it might have been caused by the trial drug. A receptionist led him directly to the main conference room and seated him in a chair at a long table.

From the looks of things, Alexander's business was thriving. The room had luxurious carpeting, a stone fireplace, and famous paintings hung on two walls. The centerpiece in the room was a large, solid-teak table. Around it were eight matching tall-backed chairs with seats, covered in burgundy leather.

The receptionist brought hot coffee. Five minutes later, the door opened and a very well-dressed Alexander Snow entered the room, with a manila folder tucked under his arm.

"Good morning, Dr. Rolland. How can I be of help?" Alex said on his way to the head of the table.

"I'd like to…well, I'm looking for legal advice concerning the death of a friend. I believe you know her." He cleared his throat. "Her name was Fawn Juzel. She died suddenly three days ago and has been buried."

"Oh, Fawn Juzel. I recall her being at our party a while back. She seemed happy and healthy then.

I'm sorry to hear of her death," Alex said, leaning back in his chair. "How can I be of help to you?"

"I need to know how to get Fawn's body exhumed. Her body needs to be autopsied by a medical examiner who isn't connected to Oregon Hospital and Science University."

Alex placed his elbow on the table, rubbed his chin with his left index finger and said, "Why wasn't an autopsy done before her burial? And why do you want her autopsied now?"

"No one in the family thought of having an autopsy done because it was assumed that Fawn died as a result of an advanced stage of cancer. However, we need a medical examiner to verify whether or not her kidneys, abdomen, et cetera contain our research trial drug."

"Dr. Rolland, are you suggesting that she was administered a trial drug that was in the animal-research stage?"

"That's exactly what I'm suggesting."

"I see." Alex's eyes were animated as they peered over the spectacles that he'd adjusted, wearing them low on the bridge of his aquiline nose. "I have to tell you that courts usually do not allow exhumation unless there are substantial and compelling reasons to do so. Three general principles govern the law of disinterment in the United States. First, it is presumed that a decently buried body should remain undisturbed where it was placed, unless good reason is given to disturb it. Second, disinterment is considered a private concern between the immediate family and the cemetery. Third, if there is a disagreement among close

153

relatives, then the matter is adjudicated by a court of equity." He paused. "I'll draw up the necessary legal documents for the appropriate family member to sign, if he or she is willing."

"If the autopsy reveals the presence of out trial drug, what's the next step?"

"I'm afraid you'll have a criminal case to deal with."

"Would you be willing to represent the family?"

"Absolutely." He paused, a puzzled look on his face. "Off the record, who do you think would do such a thing?"

"Three of my colleagues, and I believe that Dr. Karl Gunner might be the person responsible. He was her primary physician and made numerous visits to the research lab to ask about our drug trial. Dr. Gunner also knew when we first administered the trial drug, and he frequented the lab and spent time observing the rabbits' behaviors."

"Dr. Rolland, before you get ahead of yourself, let's first address the issue of body exhumation." A smile lit up Alex's face, making it clear why people liked him and why his firm had thrived. "Make an appointment with my secretary to pick up the necessary documents. Take them to a member of Ms. Juzel's family with power of attorney over her affairs, or ask that family member to come here and sign the documents. Once the documents are signed, we can have the exhumation done. If the medical examiner finds the trial drug in her body, as you seem to think he will, then we will contact the authorities, who will proceed with an investigation. Is there anything else at this time?"

"No." Silas paused with a far-off look in his eyes. "I appreciate you agreeing to represent the family and me. Thank you."

When Silas left Alex's office, he drove to the hospital. He needed to let Jessica know about his visit with Alex and discuss how to approach

Ann, Fawn's sister, about exhuming the body. He hoped Jessica would accompany him when they met with Ann. He knew a conversation about exhuming the body of her sister would be very stressful for the latter, and Jessica's support might be necessary.

Silas paged Jessica when he arrived at the hospital's coffee shop. Fifteen minutes later, she entered the coffee shop and saw him sitting at a table slowly rotating his coffee cup, deep in thought.

"Hi, Silas, what's up?"

"Jessie, I need your help. I spoke with Alex, and he told me that the process of exhuming a body can sometimes be difficult if family members of the deceased oppose the exhumation, or if there are religious prohibitions against the practice." His nervous fingers betrayed his anxiety. "Alexander also said that a court would order an exhumation as part of a criminal investigation if additional evidence were needed. But in this case, an autopsy would be the only evidence there would be to establish a criminal case."

"Okay, how can I help?" Jessica asked calmly.

"Jessie, it's important that you come with me and ask Ann Lake to sign a legal document granting permission to exhume the body. We need to prove that Dr. Gunner administered the trial drug, and the first step of that is to prove that the trail drug was administered. We need an autopsy."

"All right, when do you want me to meet with her?"

"This afternoon. This needs to be done as quickly as possible before the body deteriorates. The procedure may take a few days. My only hope is that she gives permission. I'll be setting up an appointment with Alex to review our findings as soon as we obtain them."

They were finishing coffee when Max walked in, pulled up a chair and asked, "What's the latest?"

Silas replied, "Mr. Snow will review the autopsy report when we obtain it, and decide if the evidence warrants legal proceedings. It occurred to me also, that a handwriting specialist needs to evaluate the note written in the margin of Fawn's chart and compare it to other notes on her chart written by Dr. Gunner."

They were about to leave when Dr. Gunner walked in and ordered coffee and a doughnut. As he waited for his order, he looked around and spotted the trio. In a loud voice, he said, "I need to talk with you folks."

Waving his hand, he picked up his doughnut and coffee and walked to their table.

He pulled up a chair, sat down and said, "Well, this is a cozy gathering. Dr. Rolland, what's new in research?"

Silas glanced at Max and Jessica. "Nothing."

"Come on, you must have started on a new trial. Can't imagine Seth doing nothing."

"Come off it," Max said, showing his first sign of irritation. "Sometimes things just don't work out. Like the rabbit trial."

Gunner turned and glared at Max. "You mean errors occurred? What happened?"

"They're failures, not errors, Karl."

Karl's face turned red, eyes wide. He snapped, "I don't fail. Or make errors. How the hell do you think I got to be Chief of Surgery and Chairman of the Board of one of the biggest and most important hospitals in the state? Because I've got a good mind and I am knowledgeable, and don't forget it." His mouth was tight.

"Karl, there's no need to be defensive. We're not discussing your achievements, your intelligence, or your bravado," Max said. He looked at Jessica and said, "I think it's time to get back to work." The three of them got up and left.

Max walked Jessica to the elevator and said, "That man frustrates me to no end." Then he sighed, looked at her and smiled lovingly. "Would you like to go to a movie this weekend?"

"What time?"

He kissed her gently and said, "I'll find out and call you later."

Silas dashed toward the elevator and rode the elevator with Jessica to the surgical floor, where she picked up her satchel and left with him to meet with Ann.

Jessica said, "She'll need a lot of emotional support in dealing with exhumation and giving permission for an autopsy. Be prepared, though. Even with support, she may not agree to any of this."

Accompanied by Jessica, Silas drove to Fawn's home. He told Jessica she was right. "Ann might not agree to an autopsy, and if she doesn't, Gunner would never be brought to justice." He talked about Fawn, about the laughter in her eyes, about her face beaming with joy at watching her son grow.

Fawn had lived on the outskirts of the city in a middle-class area. The house had been recently painted beige and trimmed the color of milk, and the scent of freshly cut grass permeated the air. They knocked on the front door, and Ann opened it. Fawn's 5- year old son stood behind his aunt's back and peeked around her thigh with big brown eyes. He was slender and tall for his age with a mop of black curly hair.

"Hello, big boy," Jessica said. "Can you tell me your name?"

He grinned a little and said, "Caleb."

"That's a nice name, Caleb."

Ann invited them in and sent Caleb to the playroom to play with his new blocks.

The first order of business was to ensure that everything they discussed would be kept confidential. Ann agreed to that. Only then did Silas tell her that Fawn's death might have been due to the administration of a trial drug that was still being tested on animals.

"Who gave her the drug?" Ann asked, her voice an octave higher than normal and her eyes wide.

"We think it was her doctor. To prove this, however, we need an autopsy performed. We are asking you to sign legal papers to exhume Fawn's body."

"Fawn is gone. This won't bring her back to life. God wouldn't want her disturbed, and God will punish the person who did this to her," Ann said, tears in her eyes.

Silas glanced at Jessica and then said to Ann, "Please think about this." He stood, stepped toward her and placed his hand gently on her shoulder. "I understand that this is a very difficult thing to do. But this could be your chance to bring this man to justice and ensure that he never hurts another family." He paused, looked around, and realized that Jessica had left the room. "I'll get in touch with you in a day or two. Thanks for listening."

Silas walked around the corner to the playroom and found Caleb and Jessica building a castle with his blocks. Jessica said, "Caleb, I love your castle. It's big and strong, just like you." Then, she looked around, spotted Silas and Ann looking at them, and told Caleb, "I have to go now, okay? I'll see you soon."

Jessica stood up, gave Ann a hug, and they left.

CHAPTER TWENTY FOUR

D r. Gunner left the hospital and drove to a nearby tavern he visited frequently. He sat in a corner, ignoring the other patrons, and drank three Bombay Blue Sapphire gin martinis on the rocks.

One of the other patrons was Max, who had stopped in for a quick beer. Max was not a regular, and when he saw Gunner in the corner he decided he would never become one. However, he did feel fortunate to be there to overhear the man mumbling about Fawn and drugs and investigations. Moving closer, but still saying out of direct sight, he listened closely.

By now, Gunner's speech was slurred. He was jabbering about "Silas…" "I'll tell 'em Silas…And Dr. Ponytail." Finally, the bar manager sat down with Gunner and as gently as possible asked Gunner to leave. Gunner gazed at him with glassy eyes, stood on unsteady feet, and left the premises without another word. Max went home and immediately called Silas to warn him that Gunner might try to implicate him in Fawn's death. And Silas immediately called Jessica to report what Max had heard. All three now realized their fate might well hang on the decision by Ann to allow, or prevent, Fawn's autopsy.

Three anxious days passed before Silas received a phone call at work. When he answered, a muffled sound continued for a few moments and then someone asked, "Is this Dr. Silas Rolland?"

"Yes. Whom am I speaking with?"

"This is Fawn's sister, Ann. I wanted to be certain it was you, since you asked me to keep this a secret. Yesterday, I had a conversation with a priest from the local parish. We talked for a long time and discussed exhumation, and he read me passages about life and death from the Bible. He was very helpful. During our conversation, he mentioned the sixth commandment: *Thou shalt not kill.* That suddenly made me realize that Fawn would want justice to be served." She paused. "Where do I go to give approval for exhumation? I believe this is what my sister would've wanted."

Silas breathed a sigh of relief. "I'll call Mr. Snow, the attorney, and set up a time for tomorrow. Remember, this is still highly confidential." Silas exhaled with another deep sigh. "Thank you, Ann."

He replaced the receiver gently and leaned back in his soft chair, puzzling over how much of what had happened should be shared with Seth. He knew he had to tell the man everything sooner or later, though. *It's best if I do it now,* he thought. He called Jessica, who agreed to meet him in Seth's office right away.

The two of them found Seth in his office.

"Seth." Silas paused, and then continued. "What I'm about to tell you is in the strictest confidence. You need to know the events of the past few days."

Seth looked up with a concerned expression and said with his characteristic querulousness, "All right, all right, what's the big secret?"

"Dr. Brown, Jessica, and I suspect that Dr. Karl Gunner is responsible for Fawn's sudden death. So far our evidence points to him."

"You think he killed her? How?" Seth's eyes were wide.

"We think he injected Fawn with the AVD 7008 trial drug we used on the rabbits."

"Why would he do such a thing? That's a criminal offense."

"On Fawn's medical chart, written in the margin, was our trial drug name, AVD 7008. No one, absolutely no one, knew this name except you and me. I made copies of the chart along with Gunner's notes on Fawn's and sent them to a handwriting expert to be analyzed. Also, we are awaiting the exhumation of Fawn's body, so we can have an independent medical examiner perform an autopsy. We need to know whether the drug is present in her liver, abdomen or kidneys or in other body organs."

"My God, Silas, this could ruin us," Seth said. "I can't believe Karl messed with our trial drug." Seth lowered his head, deep in thought. "You know, the more I think about it, there were several occasions where I noticed that the vials containing the AVD 7008 had less remaining serum than expected after I withdrew the proper dose for the rabbits. I did make a notation in my files of the differences. It's possible that Karl may have extracted small amounts over a period of time, since he frequented this place. He certainly had the opportunity."

Early the next Monday morning, Gunner appeared in the

research lab wearing sneakers and a jogging suit. He rushed up to the secretary at her desk and demanded to know whether Seth had come to work already. He was gasping and short of breath. He was so out of breath, in fact, that the secretary asked him to sit and brought him a glass of water.

He downed the water in three gulps. "That's better," he said. "Now, is Seth in?"

"Yes, he's in the back dealing with the surviving rabbits—the ones that received the placebo."

Gunner, with hands folded into his armpits, strutted toward Seth and barked, "I'm here to ask what exactly you know about Fawn's body being exhumed."

"Karl, I haven't heard anything like that," Seth lied and put on an expression of shock. "Why would her body be exhumed? And why are you still concerned about Fawn's death? It was cancer, wasn't it? People die of cancer."

There was an icy silence in the room. Then Karl changed the topic entirely. "My leg has been bothering me lately—the one I injured in Vietnam and again in the accident."

"Well then, you need to go home and take care of it," Seth said.

"I intend to," Gunner stared at Seth. "See you around," he said and turned to leave.

Silas and Jessica had been in the hallway during much of this conversation, and they scattered as Gunner came out of the research area. Jessica managed to conceal herself behind a nurses' station, but Silas was not so fortunate.

"You get back to your work," commanded Gunner. It was such

an abrasive tone from such an unprincipled man that Silas, without meaning to, stiffened and replied as derisively. "Perhaps *you* need to get back to work."

Just then, the phone rang on the secretary's desk, and she answered it. She listened and said, "Just one moment, sir. I'll put you on hold." She stood and announced, "Dr. Rolland, the medical examiner is on line two."

Silas walked to his desk and picked up his receiver. "Hello, this is Dr. Rolland."

"This is Dr. Dark, the medical examiner. I'm going to mail your attorney the results of the autopsy, unless you prefer to pick up the reports."

Silas saw that Gunner had now come back into the research area and was standing by the secretary's desk listening to his conversation. Jessica, intensely curious, was now standing at the door as well. "Just go ahead and mail them to me at the research lab," Silas said in as much noncommittal fashion as he could manage. "Thanks for your help."

Gunner took a step toward Silas. "What was that all about?"

Silas looked at him with dead eyes. "We're doing follow-ups on our dead rabbits. Nothing that would concern you." He turned abruptly, stepped into one of the lab rooms and closed the door.

CHAPTER TWENTY- FIVE

High clouds swept across the sky, the morning sunshine showing in slivers between them. *A pleasant day,* Jessica thought when she peered out her bedroom window at 5:30 that morning. It was early, even for her, and her body ached all over. She was exhausted from long days in surgery. She stepped into the bathroom, and moments later the telephone rang. She hoped it was someone with good news.

It was Silas. "Jessie," he said, "I'm glad you answered."

"Who else did you think would answer? Cheyenne is still sound asleep. So is Finny. What's up?"

"I know it's early, but can we meet in an hour? In the coffee shop?"

"Can we make it two hours? Remember, I have Finny to take care of first. Call Max, too, and I'll see you in two hours." She hung up before he could respond.

In the shower, she thought of Silas. *What kind of father might he make? Maybe not so good.* He always wants things to go his way, and that rarely happens when you have someone else's best interests at heart. And then there was also his reaction to her rape. He had seemed to accept it, but then his attitude toward her had become…well, more aloof. With a great deal of effort, she was not letting the rape define her. He shouldn't, either.

The phone rang again, startling her. She got out of the shower quickly and ran to answer it. This time it was Max, saying that he had a surgical case and wouldn't be able to meet that morning. "Are you going?" Max asked.

"Yeah. I agreed to go. Don't you think you'll make it out of surgery in time? I find it more comforting when you're there."

He laughed. "I find you comforting as well. OK, I'll be there, but I might be late."

"I'll see you, then," she said.

At half past seven, Jessica and Silas met with Seth at the coffee shop to discuss Fawn's autopsy. Jessica's eyes swept the entire room, and she noticed a small number of medical students sitting at a table, their faces lit up and ready for the day's challenges. They were so early in their residency they hadn't had time yet to get tired.

Silas, with a thin smile, pulled out several sheets from a manila file folder. "Look here," he said and handed the pages to Seth. Seth, with Jessica looking over his shoulder, read that the Medical Examiner had done drug studies on the remains. He had also done a methodical analysis of fluid taken from blisters on her body. Seth read the last sentence aloud. "Fawn Juzel's death was due to numerous cancerous tumors. Her liver and lungs contained the trial drug AVD 7008 along

DO NO HARM

with the chemotherapy drugs used for treatment."

At that moment, Max arrived. Silas repeated, "Fawn Juzel's liver and lungs contained the trial drug AVD 7008."

Seth, Jessica and Max all sat there and looked at each other. Then Max pulled out a packet of cigarettes, lit one up and exhaled a huge puff of smoke through his nose. "I'm not trying to be unsympathetic or difficult, but I wonder if this evidence will hold up in court."

"What do you mean?" Jessica asked.

"Well, the cause of death was multiple malignant tumors throughout her body. Even though the trial drug probably was a contributing factor in hastening her death, it's not what killed her."

Silas saw his point. He shifted his body several times, blew out a sigh and said, "What about the handwritten note on Fawn's chart? The handwriting analyst said that was Gunner's handwriting."

"And what about the shortage of the trial drug in the vials?" Seth added.

"I don't know if that will be enough evidence to convict Gunner," Max said, "but I'm sure Mr. Alexander Snow, attorney at law, will have an educated opinion." He glanced at his watch, and said, "I've a case pending in twenty minutes." He stood, stepped behind Jessica, and whispered in her ear, "I'll call you later." He looked at the others and said, "See you all later, and good luck!"

Seth said, "Let's set up a time with Mr. Snow, present our information, and hope we can get to the bottom of this mess." He looked at his watch and said, "My goodness, it's time for me to get to work as well." He stood and left.

Silas was left with the task of arranging a time with Alex to review

166

the evidence. From his office in the research lab, he made the call to the lawyer's office and set up an appointment for himself, Seth, Jessica, Max and the immediate family on Friday at ten in the morning.

When he told Seth about the appointment, Seth was pleased. "Good," he said. "I'll be happy to get this over with. Thanks for doing this, Silas. You know, never in my life would I have suspected someone of doing something like this, especially Karl."

Twenty minutes later, Seth heard a commotion outside his office. He opened the door and was face-to-face with Dr. Gunner. The man was bellowing. "Seth, you know damned well I'm important to this hospital. I devote my time and resources to the betterment of humanity. I cannot believe you've turned on me. "

"Karl, what in God's name are you talking about?" Seth's voice was cold. He was shocked that news about Fawn's exhumation would have reached Gunner's ears this soon. As he searched for what else to say, he saw Silas approaching.

"What's all this ruckus?" were the first words out of Silas's mouth, delivered in a deadly monotone.

Gunner turned, his faced red and his eye wide, and shouted, "You!" He pointed at Silas. "You're the one who killed my patient. Don't bother denying it. I will prove it in court!" He turned and rushed out, slamming the door behind him.

CHAPTER TWENTY- SIX

The weather was still a bit nippy at 10:00 in the morning on Friday when Silas, Seth, Jessica and Ann Lake reached the law offices of Alexander Snow. The waiting area was warmer and quieter, with rays of sunlight streaming through the windows. After a few moments, a receptionist came and led them all to the main conference room and served them coffee. Alexander arrived a moment later with a leather folder tucked under his arm.

"Let's get started," he said as he seated himself at the head of the table. He removed papers from the folder and placed them in front of him. "So," he continued, "the trial drug AVD 7008 was found to be present in the liver and lungs. I also received the confirmation from the handwriting analyst that Dr. Gunner's handwriting on the chart is identical to the writing of the drug name in the chart margin."

He sat erect, his hands folded on the table. "Is there anything else that anyone here can contribute to this case?"

"Yes," Seth said, frowning. "Didn't you get the statement I mailed three days ago saying that two milliliters of the trial drug were missing over a short period of time?"

Alexander shuffled through more papers, picked up a sheet and read from it while his fingers tapped on the table. "Got it here," he said, "but what proof do you have that Dr. Gunner removed that amount from the vials?"

"We keep logs of everyone who enters the lab, including arrival and departure times."

"That's good, but it doesn't prove Dr. Gunner extracted the drug from the vials. Additionally, no one saw him actually administering the drug to Fawn." He closed his eyes for a second and then opened them and said, "We can't prosecute on speculation. And, unfortunately, there isn't enough evidence to be sure to convict him."

Silas's face flushed. He glanced at Seth, and then said to Alexander, "What about having Gunner take a polygraph examination? That can tell us if he had anything to do with Fawn's death."

"At this point, law enforcement investigators haven't even acknowledged the existence of a crime yet. We need to press charges and confirm that the defendant has legal representation."

Silas shook his head and said, "Dr. Gunner told me he plans to accuse me of Fawn's murder. I can't believe a psychopath is framing me. I'm being implicated solely on the basis of a friendship with Fawn."

Jessica touched Silas's shoulder, giving him a pat she hoped was comforting.

Alexander was more comforting. "You're not being implicated in any legal fashion," he said, "so we'll worry about that if it becomes an allegation by Dr. Gunner or his attorney. Meanwhile, I'll phone the authorities and ask them to investigate. Then I'll be waiting for a police report, and for Dr. Gunner's attorney to contact me. Soon, we'll know whether the case can go to a grand jury for a criminal indictment, or to a preliminary hearing, where a judge decides if there is enough evidence to proceed. I'll keep you all informed." Alexander closed his file, stood, and left.

Back in the waiting room, Jessica spotted Leslie talking to the secretary. "Fancy meeting you in Alexander's office," she said.

"What are you doing here?" She laughed. "I guess that's a dumb thing to ask. You're probably taking your husband to lunch."

"No, but that's a good suggestion. How about we all go out to lunch? Let me pop in and ask Alex if he can come."

Seth bowed out—"Got too much to do"—and Leslie came out of Alexander's office saying he, too, had a lot on his plate. Leslie looked tired, with dark circles under her eyes. The lines on her forehead seemed more deeply etched than Jessica remembered them. She wondered what could be the matter.

At the restaurant, Leslie, with the menu in hand, looked directly at Silas and asked, "How did your meeting go?" Silas looked directly back at her and summarized what Alexander had told them.

"I'm sure Alexander will do a magnificent job." Leslie paused. "Down to the last detail. What are you ordering, Silas?" Her voice was like velvet each time she spoke to Silas.

Leslie's in love with Silas, Jessica realized. She purrs around him. This is not appropriate. It was time for her to say something. "How is your practice, Leslie? I imagine you get the experience of a lifetime, seeing all those newborns." For a second, she was a little envious of her friend. All those beautiful babies, the image flashed through her mind. She remembered when Finny was born, his eyes captivating her. Like little magnets, those eyes.

"Business is good. And yes, I do love delivering and holding those newborns. The sadness comes when mothers give their babies up for adoption."

"Where do the unwanted babies go?" Jessica asked the question as though she didn't already know.

"Most are sent to the Order of Holy Sanctuary Monastery for adoption. My understanding is that the sisters there are skilled at providing care for these little people until they are adopted."

Jessica asked casually, "Isn't Dr. Gunner on their board?"

"Yes, as far as I know. Why?"

"I saw him there when I picked Finny up from daycare. Just wondered what he was doing there."

"Who knows? He's involved in many things."

CHAPTER TWENTY- SEVEN

It was early autumn, the season of admiration for beautiful colors. Jessica arrived at the monastery to pick Finny up and was greeted by a young nun she didn't know.

"My name is Sister Teresa. How can I help?" She had big, brown eyes and looked eager to help. "I'm new here."

"I'm Dr. Tinker, and I'm here to pick my son up from daycare."

"What's his name?"

"Finny Tinker."

Sister Teresa picked up a folder from the corner desk and scanned the pages looking for Finny's name. "He's a dark-haired, 18-month old boy?"

"Yes."

Sister Teresa went pale. "Oh, my Lord!" She made the sign of the cross. "A couple came here about four hours ago and took him. They said all the necessary papers had been signed and that Mother Superior had approved. They took him to an adoption agency."

"What?" said Jessica, and then before the sister could say another word, "Who took him? Where? What agency?" Her voice kept getting louder and louder, until she was shouting, "Who is this agency?"

Tears formed in Sister Teresa's eyes as she said, "Please, Dr. Tinker, sit down and I'll get Mother Superior. I don't know what to do, but she will."

She made a phone call and, within three minutes, two nuns appeared. The older one was the Mother Superior, whom Jessica had met months ago. The Mother's posture was rigid and her face looked like iron.

"Dr. Tinker, I'm sorry. A grave error has occurred. The youngster to be adopted was named Vinny Winkler. Sister Teresa got the names mixed up. They are so similar, and the boys are even the same age and look very much alike. She paused, "We will immediately take care of this."

Jessica moved forward until she was standing within inches of the Mother Superior. "And how are you going to do that?"

"We acknowledge our error," the Mother replied calmly. "We will call the adoption agency and check on the status of the adoption."

"What agency is that?"

"It's called the *Love Me Agency*. Also, I will notify the police." she said in soft voice.

"When?"

"I will call the police immediately and notify the director of our board."

"Call the police now, and to hell with the director. Every minute, every second counts."

The Mother Superior nodded, still calm, and then disappeared around the corner to make the phone call. When she returned ten minutes later, she said, "The police officers will be here shortly. They need detailed information from you. Please sit down, Dr. Tinker," she gestured with her hand.

But Jessica couldn't just sit down. She paced back and forth, trying with trembling hands to rub away a headache that had suddenly developed into blinding pain. Suddenly, she was nauseous. "Where's the bathroom?"

Jessica rushed to the bathroom, splashed water on her face, tried—and failed—to get a grip on her emotions, and then rushed back to where the Mother Superior was still standing. Just then, two officers arrived. One, a large man with thinning gray hair, extended a hand and introduced himself as Sergeant Lief. The other, also large, stood aside and scanned the monastery grounds curiously.

Sergeant Lief asked Jessica for Finny's full name, age, a detailed description of his appearance, and whether he had any significant birthmarks. He then asked the Mother Superior about the time Finny had been handed over to the couple from the adoption agency, the agency address and the name of the person operating the agency.

Jessica handed each officer a card listing her home phone and pager number. She interrupted the sergeant's questions several times saying, "I want him found immediately."

"We'll do our job of investigating immediately, Dr. Tinker."

Then he asked Jessica one more question: "Dr. Tinker, did you at any time discuss with anyone the option of finding adoptive parents for this child?"

What had until that moment remained of Jessica's self-control gave out. She heard herself hollering at the man, "What's the matter with you? Why would I give my only love away? I want you to look for him now!" She realized she needed the man's help, though, and she wasn't going to get much cooperation about of him by yelling at him. So calmed herself down and said, "I'm sorry."

Then she was sick again, barely making it to the bathroom, then to her car, and then home where another violent wave of nausea swept over her. She was so sick, so very sick. Her stomach was wrenched into knots.

Luckily, Cheyenne was home. "What's wrong, Jessica? Shall I call 9-1-1?"

"No. No." Tears flooded Jessica's eyes. She couldn't see. Wiping her cheeks with the back of her hand, she wailed, "Finny is missing. The sisters handed him over to some sort of adoption agency by mistake." She sat on the floor, choking.

Cheyenne, with a horrified look, hurriedly paged Max and told him there was an emergency. "Jessica is very sick. Please come now if you can—hurry." She then hurried to the drugstore to pick up something for nausea.

Max arrived at her apartment door and let himself in using a key Jessica had given him. Once inside, he hollered "Jessica?" No one answered, so he checked the living room, kitchen, and bedroom. Stepping into the bathroom, he went wide-eyed when he saw Jessica lying on the floor sobbing.

"Oh, Jessica, my dear!" He picked her up and carried her to the sofa and sat beside her. "Tell me what happened."

"Max... the sisters at the monastery told me Finny was handed over to an adoption agency by mistake," she wailed.

"What?! Have you called the police?"

"No, but the sisters did while I was there. They interviewed both the Mother Superior and me about Finny."

Taking matters into his own hands, Max called the police station and talked with a sergeant who answered the phone. He had barely launched into the tale of what had happened to Finny when the sergeant interrupted, "Dr. Brown," he said, "I can assure you that we are actively involved in searching for this child."

"Sir," Max said firmly. "What if this is some sort of fraudulent scheme? What if he's sent out of the country? Children sold to orphanages are often shipped overseas. This child is like my very own, and his mother is in despair."

"That's understandable, and I'm sorry, but I can promise you that the investigation will continue until we find him. We are prompt in responding to this type of situation."

Max hung up and seated himself again next to Jessica. The smallest hint of a smile tweaked the turned-down corners of his mouth. "We will get Finny back," he said firmly. "Whoever took him will be found."

"Can you stay awhile?" Jessica asked, tears still rolling down her cheeks.

"Don't cry, Jessica," Max said, holding her tightly. "Everything will work out. I know it. I'll stay with you as long as you need." He knew this would give Jessica some reassurance. He could only hope it was the truth.

It was very late that evening when the Mother Superior called

Dr. Gunner's office. He'd encouraged her to phone whenever a critical situation occurred, regardless of time. On the second ring, he answered. "This is Dr. Gunner speaking." His words were harsh. When he found out who was calling, he said, "It's well past eight in the evening. What's the emergency?"

"A few hours ago, the wrong child was handed over to the *Love Me Agency*. The child's mother is frantic and wants him back immediately. I called the police to investigate and see if he can be located and returned."

"You called the police?" he yelled, sounding angry. "What's the matter with you? Your instructions are to inform me first, no matter what."

"Dr. Gunner, there's no need to be rude," she said. "I believe I did the right thing."

He ignored her and asked, "Did you notify the agency?"

"I tried several times, but no one has answered."

"I'll handle this situation. What is the name of the child who was taken and the name of the mother?"

His question was answered. "Dr. Tinker?" he asked, "the surgeon at Oregon Health Science University?"

"I believe that is her place of employment."

"Is Dr. Tinker still there?"

"No, she left several hours ago."

"I will handle this matter. You need not call again."

Gunner hung up and immediately called Antony Scolari. No one, however, answered the call.

CHAPTER TWENTY- EIGHT

It was a cold autumn morning, blanketed by gray clouds. Jessica awoke, but had difficulty opening her eyes after so many hours of crying. She padded the plump quilt next to her to check if Max was there, turned her head, and saw no one. She imagined all sorts of scenarios about where Finny might be and how to get him back. Her conversation with the Mother Superior was still vivid. She needed to find her little boy. She needed to demand that somebody take action.

After showering and downing a quick cup of strong, black coffee, she pulled on a pair of slacks and a sweater and threw on a jacket. Just before leaving, she noticed a note taped to the door. It was from Max saying that he would do everything he could to help her find Finny. Reading the message stirred her heart. She thought Max must be the most understanding and supportive man in the world. She tucked the note into her pocket and drove to the police station.

She arrived at the missing persons' division at half past eight, and asked to speak with the sergeant in charge. Sergeant Lief appeared and shook her hand. "Dr. Tinker, I am aware that your son is missing." He paused. "I'm also aware that he was mistakenly handed over to the *Love Me Adoption Agency* late yesterday afternoon. We called the agency last night and no one answered." He paused again. "Then we had a patrolman drive to the agency. No one answered the door."

Jessica took a deep breath and met the narrowed gaze of the solid policeman who stood before her. "What do the police plan to do next?" she asked.

"We are searching for the person or persons who operate the adoption agency."

Jessica replied, "I trust that you will inform me immediately of any new developments," to which Sergeant Lief replied, "Of course, doctor." She thanked the officer and left, feeling nauseous again.

In her car, she sat for the longest time waiting for her stomach to settle and wondering what her next move should be. Seeing a payphone outside the police station, she stepped out of the car and called Max.

"Jessica, I have a surgical case to scrub in on within minutes."

"I understand. I just want to say thanks for your kindness last evening."

"I was happy to help. I'll call you as soon as I'm out of surgery." He hung up.

Okay then, she would visit the *Love Me Adoption Agency* herself and look the place over. She looked the address up in the phone book attached to the phone booth, then located the address on a map of the city that she kept in her car.

Such irony, she thought. *An agency called* Love Me Adoption

Agency with no one to answer the phone. Who's tending to the children?

As Jessica approached the address, she saw the sign, 'Love Me Adoption Agency' with two police cars parked in front. It did not look like a good neighborhood. The building was two-story, bordered on one side by a mom-and-pop grocery store, and on the other side by an old apartment building badly in need of restoration. She drove to the end of the street, turned, and parked a short distance across the street from the building.

There, she waited to see what the police would do. Rain started to fall lightly, and she tried to distract herself by watching the raindrops roll down the car windows. Twenty minutes later, two policemen stepped outside the door followed by—Antony Scolari?! What on earth was the father of her child doing mixed up in all of this?

The officers talked to Antony, who waved his hands in the air. Jessica watched and waited. The policemen entered their car and drove off. Then Antony, taking long strides, walked to his car, got in and drove off.

Jessica followed. Halfway to the hospital, it hit her: Antony was going to see Gunner. She remembered all the times she'd seen the two of them together and wondered what they had to talk about.

Once at the hospital, Antony parked his car and dashed inside. Jessica parked her car and also entered the hospital. She took the elevator to Gunner's floor and discreetly checked the hallway, then walked to the end of the corridor. She stood there, listening carefully, without turning the corner.

She heard a door slam, and peeked around the corner. It was Antony straightening his jacket and heading toward her down the hallway. In the blink of an eye, the door opened again and Gunner called out, "Let me know the status as soon as you find out." Then, he disappeared inside again. Antony stopped and turned his head, but gave no response. Then he continued toward her.

As he neared her, she moved back a few feet, and just before he rounded the corner she turned her head, lowered her chin and pulled up her jacket collar. As he passed her by, she knew what she would do – follow him, and then confront him.

Antony left the hospital, got back in his car, and drove back to the agency. He pulled into the agency's parking lot, got out, and looked around as though he'd somehow sensed he was being followed. Jessica, already out of her car by then, barely managed to duck into the grocery store in time to avoid being seen.

Antony stepped briskly into the agency building. Jessica waited awhile before approaching the door. She knocked. Then she knocked again. The third time, she banged on the door with her fist. With that, a plump, gray-haired lady slowly opened the door. She said, "I wish to speak to the person operating this agency."

"I'm Claire, the secretary. Do you have an appointment?"

"No, I don't have an appointment, and I don't need one." She stomped toward the lady, who stepped back to get out of her way. "Where is his office?" Her words were like ice.

"Upstairs, first door on your right," Claire said with a quiver in her voice.

Jessica pushed past her and ran upstairs, taking two steps at a time. She inhaled deeply, lowered her shoulders to relax, and inhaled again slowly before entering. She opened the door without knocking--and saw Antony seated in a swivel chair and turning toward her. He smiled, showing those straight white teeth that contrasted so strikingly with his dark complexion. She knew he remembered her, even though it had been a one-night stand.

"Hello." He stood and stared at her for a moment. "It's been a long time since we met. What are you doing here?" His voice was brisk. He seemed curious rather than guilty.

"What am I doing here? What the hell do you think?" She stepped close enough to breathe on him. "I know the police have been here, and I'm here to get my son back, Finny Tinker, who was taken from the monastery."

"Are you a doctor or a nurse?" he interrupted. He seemed shocked "I've seen you at the hospital."

"Yes, I'm a surgeon, and I work at the same place as your friend, Gunner. I'm Finny's mother, and I demand you bring him back to me from wherever you're keeping him."

"Well…" He seemed baffled. "Well, I'm not sure where he is at this second."

"You better find out! Is this some kind of fraudulent, business-scheme agency?"

"Of course not. Everything is above board here. I've been working with Dr. Gunner for years. The two of us were in Vietnam together, and we own this agency."

"Bullshit! If this is legal, then where is Finny? Where are the other children?" With effort, she refrained from slapping him. "You best call your contacts and bring him here now, if you don't want to spend the rest of your life in prison. Think what that would do to your family. But then again, you probably don't give a damn."

"Prison? What the hell are you talking about?"

"Don't play cat-and-mouse with me. Legal businesses like adoption agencies know exactly where children are placed and where they are at all times." She swallowed hard. "Have you taken time to look at Finny? Of course not—you're too busy making illegal cash to line Gunner's and your pockets. Well, I want you to hear this." She paused. "You're Finny's father. Our one-night affair created him."

Antony was momentarily stunned with the revelation, but quickly recovered and said, "Come off that crap. You're not going to hang that on me."

"You want to bet? The judge will order a DNA test, and we will see. When you see him, take a closer look. I expect him to be delivered to me within 24 hours." She turned and slammed the door as she left.

On her way out, she said to the secretary, "Go to the police now and tell them what you know about my missing little boy." Then she got to her car and went to the police department to tell Sergeant Lief about her visit to the adoption agency and to learn about their latest information on Finny.

CHAPTER-TWENTY-NINE

Jessica had just completed a major surgery when her pager went off, telling her she had a phone call. It might be good news about Finny. She rushed to the phone at the nurses' station. "This is Dr. Tinker." She hoped she sounded better than she felt.

"Jessica, this is Max. Have you heard anything about Finny."

She hadn't, and she told him so, trying not to cry.

"Well, maybe soon." Max said. Then, "I'm at the construction site. You could drive over and see our new clinic. It's really coming along."

The clinic seemed very unimportant. She began to cry in earnest, now breathing audibly through a runny and congested nose. "Max," she said, "I need to hang up. Please call me later."

Max immediately called her again. When she answered, he said, "Jessica, I understand that you're very concerned about Finny. So am I. Meet me at the coffee shop in 15 minutes."

She appeared at the hospital coffee shop as instructed, but the conversation wasn't about Finny. Instead, after kissing her gently on the cheek, Max said, "Jessica, I've gotten at least four calls from Silas. He's becoming frantic about the legal situation concerning Fawn. He wants you at a meeting that Alexander set up with Seth, me and Fawn's sister."

"Max, I don't know if I can handle this now. Yesterday, I went to the *Love Me Adoption Agency*, waited in the car till the two policemen who were there left, and then walked into the building. Antony Scolari, the architect who was involved with the hospital research construction extension, is the owner of the agency. I confronted him and accused him of causing Finny's disappearance." She paused, blew her nose, and looked at Max. "You won't believe what I did next. I followed Antony to Gunner's office at the hospital. He stayed only a brief while, and Gunner yelled at him as he left saying, 'Keep me informed about the situation.' I know they discussed Finny's disappearance." Jessica couldn't bring herself to tell him that Antony was Finny's father.

"I recommend from here on out that you let the police do their investigation, Jessica." Max was serious, his look intent and unwavering. "If you interfere, they may start looking at you, instead of putting all their efforts into finding Finny."

Jessica started to object, but then she realized he was right. As hard as it was going to be, she had to just let the police to do their jobs. Sighing, she called Silas, who answered on the first ring.

"Jessie, Alexander wants the four of us to meet in his office. I really want you there."

She glanced at Max, who nodded, and said, "What time?"

"Day after tomorrow at 9:00 in the morning. At Alexander's

office."

"I'll see you there."

"Well done," Max said with a smile.

The next morning, Jessica woke in a panic. It was bad enough having her son taken, but not being able to do anything about it was even worse. Well, she could at least call her mother and let her know.

At the first ring, her mother picked up the phone. "Mother, this is Jessica." She began weeping again.

"Honey, what's wrong?"

"Oh Mother. Finny disappeared. A nun from the monastery handed him over to an adoption agency by mistake."

"Oh, God! Have the police been called?"

"Yes, the police are looking for him. They said yesterday they might have a lead as to his whereabouts. He's not at the agency, apparently. They went there. I went there, too. I have to get off the phone now. I will let you know as soon as he's found." She hung up, not able to deal with any more questions. Somehow, she got through the day; another major surgery, two patients with complications, all the sort of thing she was by now accustomed to—but not when Finny might be in danger.

Early the following morning, Jessica called the police department to inquire if they had any new information. A sergeant on the case told her they were "making headway." They "had a lead," he said. Nothing she hadn't heard before. She thanked the man and hung up. Then, she finished getting dressed and ate a chocolate chip cookie and half a slice of toast with jam, washing down the sugar with a cup of coffee. Afterwards, she left for Alexander's office.

Everyone was already seated around the conference table and

having coffee when she arrived at the meeting. "Please sit down, Dr. Tinker," Alexander said. "We are about to get started."

Jessica poured herself a cup of coffee and sat down next to Seth. She found it very difficult to concentrate on anything other than Finny, but she did try to pay attention to Alexander as he discussed what the grand jury might do about Fawn's death.

Alexander seemed completely in control, as though this were a normal day. Even under stress, Alexander always functioned as though everything were normal, a trait that occasionally drove Leslie to distraction. "If you want to keep your sanity, keep your routine," Alexander would tell her.

"Each of you will receive a witness subpoena to attend a grand jury hearing," he was saying now.

Ann immediately asked, "Will you be there to help us answer questions?"

"I can't be with any of you in a federal grand jury room," he replied. "But remember, your job is not to determine whether Dr. Gunner is guilty or not guilty of a crime. You will be asked questions only so that the jurors can determine whether there is sufficient evidence to bring criminal charges against him. When you are asked questions, you will need to speak truthfully and freely."

Silas asked, "In your opinion, is this case strong enough to go to trial?"

Alexander straightened his shoulders and cleared his throat. "I have doubts about there being enough evidence to convict Dr. Gunner of hastening Fawn's death. If the case is dismissed, there isn't much we can do." He removed his glasses, rubbed at an eye, and said, "However, the grand jury may find evidence that will move the case to a trial.

"Also," he continued, "I'm quite confident that a grand jury would determine there is very little evidence that you, Silas, or you, Seth, had anything to do with Fawn's death."

"That's comforting to know." Silas responded. He had poured out his feelings about Dr. Gunner to Alexander, and it was important to him that Alexander be on this side.

When everyone left, Jessica drove downtown to a small restaurant where she'd arranged to meet Max. She had just been seated when she realized that Dr. Gunner and two other members of the hospital board were just entering the restaurant. Her reaction was visceral; she simply fled. Then she was forced to stand in the restaurant parking lot waiting for Max. When he arrived—late—she dashed to his vehicle, got in and said almost too quickly to be understood, "Let's go elsewhere. Gunner and his colleagues are here."

They went to another restaurant nearby. When they were seated there, Max said, "Jessica, you need to get a grip on yourself. You don't want to harass Dr. Gunner. Just leave him to the grand jury and wait for everyone to testify. And also, you must trust that the police are investigating aggressively to find Finny."

"But Max, I need to find Finny now. Maybe I can return to the adoption agency and speak with Antony again." She forced herself to speak slowly enough to be understood. "I don't know about this, *Love Me Adoption Agency*. A real adoption agency would have records, but Antony didn't even check any records to see who was adopting Finny. Things just don't seem to add up."

"I strongly suggest that you don't go to the agency. The police will issue a warrant to search Antony's architect office and his adoption agency, and may even arrest him, and you don't want to get in the middle of that. They may even be there right now."

After lunch, Max drove Jessica home. He walked her to her apartment door and assured her he would call her later. "Please try to rest for the remainder of the day, alright?" he said, putting his arms around her and giving her a long, loving hug and a kiss. Her heart skipped a beat. She so needed comfort right now but had to realize that Max had become more and more essential in her life. *I must tell him about Finny's father,* she reminded herself. *Soon.*

The next morning, Jessica was at a nurses' station reviewing post-operative patients' charts, when she was approached by a man who handed her an envelope. She walked a few steps down the hallway and opened the envelope. It was the expected grand jury subpoena. She slid it back into the envelope, folded it in thirds and crammed it into a pocket in her slacks.

"Great. That's all I need—to spend time testifying instead of looking for Finny," she muttered sarcastically. She walked back to the nurses' station and found Max there, reviewing the chart for a patient he was scheduled to operate on that day.

CHAPTER THIRTY

Two days had passed when Jessica picked up the early morning newspaper outside her apartment door. The headlines read in big letters "Surgeon's Son Missing; Local Adoption Agency Suspected."

The article, which she read at her kitchen table, was no more informative than the headline, and the more she read of it, the more frustrated she got. "WHERE'S MY FINNY?!" she screamed.

It was time to go to the courthouse. After she testified, she would go once again to the police station to check on any progress the police might have made in finding Finny.

By the time she made her way through the crowded courthouse hallway to the elevator and then across an overpass to the third floor where the hearing was to be held, it was ten past ten o'clock. Five minutes to spare.

She was called into the jury room almost immediately when

she arrived. There were at least a dozen grand jurors and the district attorney already in the room, everyone somber and serious. She expected questions about Fawn's sudden death, but instead, the jurors focused on her association with Dr. Gunner over the years.

She struggled to be entirely truthful about the man, and at the same time not to reveal her intense dislike of him. She wanted to scream, to hurt him, to imprison him for violating her. It was so bad that she could taste the dirt and leaves on her mouth all over again, could almost feel the cold, wet ground he had forced her to lay on.

Finally, there were questions about Silas and about the rabbits. She took a sip of water from a glass that had been placed on a table near her, cleared her throat, and said, "Dr. Silas Rolland is a hardworking, devoted, and, above all, sincere research analyst. I believe that he ordered the exhumation of Fawn's body because her death was similar to that of the rabbits in the trial study.

"I personally witnessed the remarkable recovery of those rabbits after the trial drug, AVD 7008, was administered. Their malignant tumors disappeared." She swallowed hard and continued, "Temporarily. After several weeks, the rabbits that had received the drug suddenly died." She cleared her throat and added. "Just like what happened to Fawn."

"What about the drug and the medical chart?" she was asked. Her answer: "The name of the trial drug, AVD 7008, was written in the margin of Fawn's medical chart. Dr. Rolland had a handwriting expert compare Dr. Gunner's handwriting with the margin note, and it was identical, according to his report."

One juror asked, "To your knowledge, did Dr. Gunner have access to the drug?"

"Yes. He had access to the research lab and knew about the drug."

"Do you have any personal knowledge that Dr. Gunner entered the research lab and obtained any of this drug?"

"No, no I don't."

After a few more questions the jurors said, "Thank you doctor. You may go now."

Alexander was just outside the grand jury room. "How did it go?" he asked. "Do you have any concerns or questions for me?"

"Not really. The questions weren't as difficult as I thought they might be. Thanks for asking. I need to get to work now," she said. Better to put off visiting the police station until after work, when she would have time to wait there if the sergeant was not immediately available to speak with her. On the way to the hospital, she paged Max and asked him to meet her in the coffee shop. She could use some caffeine before seeing her patients.

The late morning news was on the television in the coffee shop. The police "were making progress." The *Love Me Adoption Agency* was "under investigation." *Still nothing new.* Jessica thought. "Oh, my God Finny, where are you?" she whispered. She couldn't just do nothing. She would go to the police station now.

At that moment, Max walked in. He frowned when he saw her standing with her satchel over her shoulder, ready to leave.

"Jessica, where are you going?" he asked her.

"Max. Oh Max," she said. "Just now, the newscaster announced that the police are closer to finding Finny. But why haven't they called me? Please come with me to the police station. I need to know what is going on." She was pulling on his arm, trying to move him toward the door.

"Jessica, let's think this over. I hope you're aware that the news media will be all over you about this breaking news. They'll follow you from the hospital to the police station, and you'll really be impeding the police in their efforts. Sit down. Have another cup of coffee, whatever you're drinking, while I have mine."

He was right again. "Okay," she said, sat down and burst into tears. She was so angry, so frightened. *I cannot lose my son,* she thought. *I cannot!*

CHAPTER THIRTY-ONE

Mid-morning several weeks later, in October, Sergeant Lief and his partner approached the *Love Me Adoption Agency* door. The sergeant straightened his posture slightly, placed his right hand on his waist, and checked his handgun holster before knocking firmly. The front door opened, and the secretary stood frozen when she saw the men. She looked pale and distraught.

"What can I do for you?"

"Sergeant Lief, Missing Person's Unit," he said, flashing his badge. "This is Detective Green. We'd like to speak to the owner."

The secretary looked wildly about before answering, "Mr. Scolari's office is downtown, in the City Architectural Building. He's probably there now."

Sergeant Lief flashed a warrant in front of her face and said, "Where are your files listing the names of adopted children?"

She pointed to a gray, metal filing cabinet.

The two officers opened the cabinet and pulled out a three-ring, expandable binder that held a four-inch thick sheaf of paper on which children's names were listed alphabetically. They scanned the names. Finny was not listed.

"Ma'am," the detective asked, "Where is Finny Tinker's name?"

The secretary looked like a rabbit caught in headlights.

"Ma'am," the detective repeated. "Where can we find Finny Tinker's name? We need to know where and by whom he was adopted."

"I—I don't know." She stared at the detective, her face a blotchy red. "The agency changes the names of the children."

"What name was he given?"

She stepped toward the officers, rotated the binder toward herself, and ran her finger down the column.

"Here it is." She put her finger next to a name: Freddie Truck. "We always have their new names begin with the same letters as their original names."

"Why change the names?"

"Changing their names prevents their being traced by the birth parents later on. All agencies do this." She looked directly at the sergeant and said, "Sir, I don't know anything more. I don't know where any of these kids go from here."

"If you are lying, I will arrest you for obstruction of justice."

"I really don't know. I only work here part-time. You'll need to ask Mr. Scolari," she said.

The policemen searched the agency from top to bottom for any evidence leading to Finny's whereabouts, but found nothing. Half an hour later, they left the premises and headed to Antony Scolari's office. The building was easy to find, marked as it was by a brass plaque with 'Antony Scolari—Architect' in large type. Antony's office was just as obvious, with 'Antony Scolari—Architect' etched on the glass door.

The man himself was ensconced in an opulent office with a solid cherry wood desk, books in floor-to-ceiling bookcases and a large Monet art reproduction. It seemed almost pointless to ask, "Are you Antony Scolari?"

"Yes, I am," he answered in a guarded tone.

"I'm Sergeant Lief, and this is Detective Green. We are here to get information on the whereabouts of a child named Finny Tinker who, according to your records at the *Love Me Adoption Agency* has been adopted. By whom has he been adopted?" Sergeant Lief would have intimidated a quarterback.

"Sergeant, we arrange for the adoption of many children. I will need to review my records to answer your question." At that moment, the telephone on his desk rang. "Excuse me." He picked up the phone, and said, "Hello…yes…just keep him there…no, I repeat no, do not send him anywhere. Do you understand me?"

"Who was that call from?" Detective Green asked.

"A business associate," said Antony.

"Mr. Scolari," Lief said, "you need to come with us to your agency so that we can review your records and determine where and by whom Finny Tinker was adopted."

"Okay. Just let me get my jacket."

CHAPTER THIRTY - TWO

That morning, Jessica was dressed in surgical scrubs after finishing a case, and was writing pre-operative orders for a patient who was to be operated on the next day. She had just put down the chart when Silas rushed up.

"Can we go for a walk around the hospital?"

"No. It's cold out, and I'm not in the mood for walking. Let's go downstairs for coffee. I need a caffeine lift anyway—busy day ahead. Excuse me for a minute, though. I need to change."

Fifteen minutes later, she reappeared in a sweater and slacks that she hoped made her look curvy. She was drawn to Silas so strongly these days, even though her life was in shambles with Finny still missing. Feelings she thought had gone since their breakup had surfaced again. Those feelings, though, had no place in her current life. She kept that in mind.

Silas, however, didn't seem to notice what she looked like. "Jessie," he said on the way to the coffee shop, "The grand jury decided that there wasn't enough concrete evidence for our case to go to trial." He was silent for a moment. "Gunner must be happy. He's probably sitting at his favorite tavern, laughing his head off as we speak."

"Let it go, Silas. Fawn is gone. You're too good a person to lose sleep over this. Just imagine, with continued drug trials, you'll one day discover a cure for cancer."

When they ordered coffee and were seated, Silas said, "Jessie, I have something special to ask." Now he was noticing her. He said in a soft, low voice, "Do you think there is hope that we might re-establish out relationship? I miss you terribly. I love you."

Jessica stared at him for a moment. To herself, she repeated, *those feelings have no place now.* Silas cleared his throat and said, "I'll learn to accept and love Finny. Just give me time."

The mention of Finny's name increased Jessica's ever-present anxiety. She felt as though waves of misery were ripping at her. Realizing that Silas was waiting for an answer, though, she put her emotions aside for the moment. "Silas, too much has happened since our separation. I loved you with all my heart, but you couldn't accept me totally because I made a stupid mistake." She focused for a moment on his captivating, coal-black eyes and added, "How do I know you would keep your promise to love Finny? Every time you looked at me and Finny, tell me you wouldn't be reminded of my indiscretion."

"You just have to trust me. But I can't help but wonder if Max is part of the reason you're not giving me a second chance."

"As cold and straightforward as this may sound, I'm not in love with you anymore, I still really care about you, though, and I hope we can remain friends." Jessica realized that she hadn't said that to protect

Max, but rather to help Silas. She knew she was responsible for hurting him. She'd lied, made excuses, and even hid her pregnancy from him. Even now, it was difficult for her to deal with the guilt of her sinful behavior.

She glanced at her watch and said, "Silas, I really must go. I have a surgical case in thirty minutes." She stood, bent over, and gave him a kiss on the cheek. As she left, he continued sitting there, his head lowered.

Walking down the hallway back to surgery, Jessica took the time to take a deep breath, relax her shoulders, and quietly thank God for guiding her.

* * *

Meanwhile, Sergeant Lief and Detective Green had arrived at the adoption agency with Antony. The papers that had been strewn about during the earlier search for Finny's name were cleaned up. Presumably the secretary had done that.

Lief got those papers out again, while Green directed Antony to produce the real list, with the real names of the children and their adoptive parents."

"Fine." Antony's voice was one of resignation. He got on his knees, crept under his desk, unlocked a hidden drawer, and pulled out two medium-sized manila folders filled with paper, which he handed to the officers.

"Is there anything else you can give us?"

"No. That's it."

"Mr. Scolari, we'll be in touch with you soon. Do you need a ride to get back to your office?"

"No, I'll manage." He was hostile.

The officers took the materials, along with the earlier binders, and left. As soon as they were out the door, Antony dialed Gunner's number. After five rings, he slammed the phone into its cradle and called Gunner's hospital pager and left a message. Five minutes later, his phone rang.

When he answered, Dr. Gunner bellowed, "What do you want?"

"Karl, the police were at our adoption agency asking questions about our adoption practices. They seized the records."

"Track down that damn kid of Dr. Pigtail's and return him to her, pronto. Otherwise, they'll never let up." Gunner paused. "Oh God, what a mess! Let me know when the kid's back. Don't call me here. Call my residence. Understood?" There was another brief pause, and then Gunner said firmly, "Whatever you do, for God's sake, don't involve me." He hung up.

Antony, with phone still in hand, lost his temper. "The hell with you, Karl! Don't you dare double-cross me!"

Antony sat at his desk for hours, mulling over what to do next. It was late in the afternoon when he picked up the phone again and dialed the captain's assistant of a certain freighter in Honolulu. He requested that the children on board, especially the little boy named Finny Tinker, be held at the safe house. "Someone from the mainland would pick him up within 24 to 48 hours," he said.

The captain's assistant put him on hold for a few more minutes, then replied, "Mr. Scolari, Finny is here as you requested, but the freighter carrying the other children departed for Manila two hours ago."

"All right, just hold on to Finny."

* * *

As soon as they left, the two policemen had begun to check the seized adoption agency records. A number of the adoptive parents seemed to be in Portland, so they decided to follow up with them first.

They drove to the home of the family listed first. Arriving, they observed a middle-class, one-story home. They knocked, and the door was opened by an elderly man with gray hair and a cane. He seemed surprised to see two policemen standing in front of him. "How can I help you?" he asked.

"Sir, are you Mr. Stampe?"

"No. I'm Tim Wheater."

A woman about the same age stepped up beside the man and said, "I'm Emma Wheater, and this is my husband. What do you fellows want?" She sounded like a no-nonsense kind of woman.

"We're looking for Mr. and Mrs. Stampe. Do you have any idea where they might be?

"No, not at all," the man said. "We've lived here over 25 years, and there's never been anyone living in this neighborhood by that name."

The policemen glanced at each other, thanked the couple, and left. They went to the next home on the list. And the next. After five visits to five different homes, none of which housed the families indicated, they realized that the entire *Love Me Adoption Agency* business was bogus.

Back at the police department, they met with their supervisor and discussed the possibility that they had stumbled upon a child trafficking operation. The police chief contacted several other states where children were supposed to have been adopted and learned that the results were the same as in Portland. He then immediately notified the FBI.

When the FBI agents arrived at the Portland station, they were informed by the local police about the disappearance of Finny Tinker, and the files from the *Love Me Adoption Agency* were turned over to them. Two FBI agents drove directly to the Order of Holy Sanctuary Monastery and obtained two additional lists of children's names. One list had names of working parents who'd placed their children in daycare and the other listed children for adoption. The FBI agent asked Mother Superior which list Finny Tinker was on.

"Finny Tinker is the son of Dr. Jessica Tinker, a local surgeon. The boy was accidentally released to a couple that had always picked up children ready to be adopted. I'm so sorry this error occurred. Finny was never to be adopted. One of our new sisters mixed up the names. The boy to be adopted was named Vinny Winkler. Again, I regret the error."

With these lists in hand, the FBI agents drove to Antony Scolari's place of business. They knocked. No one answered. They turned the doorknob. It was locked. They would need a warrant to enter. Not wanting to wait long enough to get one, they drove immediately to the *Love Me Adoption Agency.*

A man appeared from around a corner and said, "May I help you?"

"Are you Antony Scolari?"

"Yes, I am." Antony had just hung up the phone after talking to the ship captain's assistant in Honolulu, who had said that he was maintaining watch over Finny at the safe house until someone from the mainland picked him up.

The officer approached Antony, flashed his FBI badge, and said,

"You're under arrest for child trafficking and operating a fraudulent business."

"What?" Antony pushed the sleeves of his sweater up to his mid-arms as if preparing for a fistfight. One of the agents took that opportunity to handcuff him.

"Where is Finny Tinker?"

Eyes wide and face pale, Antony replied, "He's at a safe house in Honolulu. I planned to send someone today to pick him up. He was being held on a freighter anchored at a port in Honolulu, along with five other children who are now on their way to the Philippines."

He was escorted into a police car and taken to jail.

At 7:00 that evening, the FBI dispatched four agents to fly to Honolulu. After picking up Finny, one of the agents would fly back to the mainland with the kid, while the other three would go on to the Philippines, board the freighter and secure the five other stolen children. The Manila Police were put on alert for the freighter's arrival in their country.

Sergeant Lief called Jessica at her home late that evening and said, "Dr. Tinker, your son, Finny, has been located in Honolulu. FBI agents are on their way to get him."

"Honolulu?! What's he doing there?"

"That is all I can tell you officially at this time. However, I will say this is a case of international child trafficking. An FBI agent will return your son to you day after tomorrow. He is unharmed. Thank you for your patience while we conducted our search for him." He hung up.

CHAPTER THIRTY – THREE

Max lived in a condominium west of the university. From the top of the hill, he had a fantastic view of the Tualatin Mountains, locally known as the "Portland West Hills." He was gazing at the view now, and wondering whether Jessica would enjoy seeing it every morning when she arose from their shared bed. With that thought, he left for the hospital.

He parked in the designated doctors' area and killed the engine. It was still relatively dark in the early morning, and the canopy of a sprawling oak tree over the car blocked the light from the lamppost outside the parking garage. He took the time, in the semi-darkness, to wonder if Jessica might consider marrying him after she got Finny back—if she got Finny back. He entered the hospital and stopped at the coffee shop for a 16-ounce cup of strong coffee. Jessica was surprisingly there as well, getting her own coffee.

"Hi," she said and put her arm around his waist.

"Hi." He glanced at his watch and said, "Good God, how come you're here so early?" He turned and gave her a good look—and realized she was radiant.

"The police called last night and said they found Finny in Honolulu and will bring him home in the next two days. He's okay. They said he's okay." She paused. "The FBI is now involved in this situation.

"Really?! That's great news!" exclaimed Max, then a confused expression passed on his face. "Why would the FBI be involved?"

"They think they have a case of national and international child trafficking. Antony Scolari, that architect who owned the adoption agency, provided the information they needed to find the kids. Oh, Max, I can hardly wait to hold my sweet Finny again!"

"Me too. This morning's newspaper headlines were all about Finny's disappearance and what happened to him. You'll be swamped with reporters hammering you for the latest information." He squeezed her shoulders and added, "I'll bet you stayed awake most of the night worrying about Finny, so why don't you take the day off?"

"Oh, Max, you're very understanding. I'll follow your medical recommendation." She chuckled and said, "Is your day busy?"

"I've been inundated with surgery cases and demands from our clinic construction supervisor, Jessica. Would you like to come with me later this afternoon and check out the building? I think you'll be surprised at how nice it is." He looked down at her, brushed his fingers under her chin, and smiled.

"Yes, I'll be ready. What time?"

"I'll pick you up at four...your place." He gave her a kiss and said, "Go home. Do something nice for yourself."

Jessica smiled. *How protective of this man,* she thought. *And how kind.* Both he and Finny will be so excited to be reunited.

Taking her coffee with her, she headed toward the nurses' station to check out for the day.

"Well, well, if it isn't Dr. Ponytail." It was Gunner. "So, you told the grand jury a pack of lies about me. Without any evidence."

Jessica felt as though she were being attacked by a snarling bulldog trained to kill and eager to take a chunk out of somebody. "Dr. Gunner," she said, "I don't wish to engage in an argument with you, and as of this moment, all I am is concerned for my son. Good day." She walked away.

CHAPTER THIRTY-FOUR

ntony Scolari had been booked into the Multnomah County Jail in Portland. An FBI agent entered his cell and looked him over from head to toe. "Your yellow-orange jumpsuit is becoming." he said, with one corner of his upper lip raised.

"What do you want? I told you where Finny Tinker is."

"If you understand the gravity of this situation, you'll tell us every detail about your adoption business. You'll tell us who is connected with this operation. And I mean *everyone*. Every person involved from a large degree to a lesser degree. Otherwise, you know as well as I do that you don't have much hope of ever getting out of prison." There was a long silence and the agent said, "Think about all this." Then, he left.

Early the next morning, Antony requested permission from the guard at the jail to call his attorney. "A damned good lawyer," he muttered, "who'll know the legal alternatives, if there were any."

Several hours later, his attorney arrived, pen in hand and carrying a shiny black leather briefcase. "Well, Mr. Scolari," he said, "What can I do for you?"

"I need to know what the FBI want. I've told them the whereabouts of Finny Tinker."

"Well, from what I've read in the newspaper and from what I've heard… the evidence is against you. Let me outline the possibilities: you could be in prison a long time, or you could be in prison even longer than that. I strongly recommend you tell the truth about all the people involved in these criminal activities. If you plead guilty and be very forthcoming, we may be able to ask for a plea bargain and get you a lenient sentence." The attorney waited, his eyebrows raised. Antony said nothing. "Seriously," he said then, "give this some thought and let me know tomorrow how you want to proceed."

"Will you let me know if the doctor gets her boy back?" Antony asked. "I'm sorry about Finny getting taken, and about the other children being sent away."

"Out of personal interest, Mr. Scolari, do you have children?" asked the attorney.

"Yes, I do. A boy and a girl." Antony looked ravaged.

After breakfast the next day, several FBI agents entered Antony's cell prepared for an interrogation. Silence reigned, painful silence, until his attorney arrived 10 minutes later.

"Okay," Antony said without preamble. "I'll sign an agreement for a plea bargain."

A conversation ensued between the attorney and the FBI agents, about how much information known by Antony might be worth, and how many years that might mean. The attorney nodded, and the interrogation began.

"Mr. Scolari, this conversation will be taped. How did you come up with this scheme for child trafficking?"

"I didn't. While I was serving with the armed forces in Vietnam, I befriended a doctor. He kept telling me we could both become wealthy if we didn't get killed. He was the one who actually conceptualized the entire plan." Antony took a sip of water from a plastic glass placed on the table next to him.

"Was this a Vietnamese doctor?"

"God, no. It was Dr. Karl Gunner. Gunner teaches at the university here and sits on the hospital board. He also sits on the board of the Order of Holy Sanctuary Monastery. But… but the sisters didn't know that our agency was child trafficking."

The attorney whispered to himself, "My God! The monastery… a place of innocence ruled by corruption. A godly place ruled by the ungodly."

"How much money did you make?" the agent asked, bending forward slightly.

"Quite a lot," Antony said, proud of himself for a second, and then not proud at all. He paused, looked at his attorney, who motioned for the questions to proceed.

"How did you invest your money?"

Antony took a deep breath and said, "We both put our money into Swiss banks and other banks in the Cayman Islands. We also invested here, in the agency itself. And we improved our homes." He paused, then added, "And in stocks, a diversified portfolio."

The agent pushed a piece of paper across the table and handed Antony a pen.

"Please write down the names of all the people who profited from your scheme."

"Fine." For several minutes, Antony wrote down names, frowned, wrote down more names, and frowned some more. "That's all I can remember," he said finally.

"Now, Mr. Scolari, you understand you will be prosecuted in a court of law?"

"Yes. I just want you to know that I don't know where many of the children went, or what happened to them over the years."

Altogether, the interrogation took several hours. On the way out, the FBI agent said, "That was some confession."

"Yes, it was," replied the attorney.

CHAPTER THIRTY-FIVE

Jessica bolted out of bed apprehensive, weeping, and disoriented. The ringing of the telephone in the kitchen had awakened her. She'd dreamt that Finny was lost forever.

Quickly regaining composure, she threw on a robe and went flying out of the bedroom into the kitchen, grabbing the phone out of its cradle.

"Hello?"

"Is this Dr. Tinker?"

"Yes, yes it is."

"This is Detective Sharon Mayo from the FBI. Your son, Finny, is with me at this moment, and I'd like to bring him to you now. Is that possible?"

"Oh, absolutely! How is he?"

"He's fine."

"Oh, oh yes! I'll be here waiting for him. Do you have my address?" Jessica was ecstatic.

"Yes I do, and I'll bring him over within the hour."

Jessica immediately called Max. She knew it was his day off, and that he was probably still sleeping.

"Hello?" His voice sounded groggy.

"Max, please don't be upset with me for calling you so early. I know you were on call last night, and you're probably exhausted. But Finny will be here sometime in the next hour. Max, can you come over now? I need you. Finny will want to see you." She paused for a breath. "Please?"

"Oh! Okay. Make us some strong coffee, and I'll be at your place as soon as I can get there."

Within the hour, there was a knock on the door. She ran and swung the door open. "Max!" No

Finny yet. "Come in please." She stepped toward him and gave him a hug, then said, "I'll pour you a cup of coffee." Her voice rang out. He hadn't heard her like this in far too long. It was like music to his ears.

He pulled her close before she could turn away. The fluidity of the movement took her by surprise. He didn't try to kiss her, didn't make any advances; just held her tight, and rubbed his hand down her back, as though he knew how much she needed it – the contact, the connection. She needed him.

He put his arm around her shoulder and then actually took her pulse. "Jessica," he whispered, "You need to settle down before Finny comes. You don't want to scare him. Now, let's have a cup of coffee."

Max had such an acute sense of what was needed. And he had such a calm, clear mind. "Oh, Max, what would I do without you?" she exclaimed. "You're an angel! Thanks for coming and being with me."

"I'm looking forward to seeing Finny, too, you know," he said. "Oh, I'll bet Cheyenne will be happy to see him, as well. Is she still sleeping?

"Yes. I peeked into her bedroom earlier, and she's sound asleep. I'm sure Finny will wake her up."

Ten minutes later, the doorbell rang and Jessica ran to answer it. There was Finny! He stared at Jessica with his big brown eyes, and then lifted up his arms toward her crying with joy, "Mama! Mama!"

Jessica scooped him up. Tears ran down her cheeks; so much for her attempt to be calm. She kissed him and kissed him and kissed him. Finally, Finny ducked his head. Enough kissing. He looked over, spotted Max, and began to wiggle. Jessica put him down and he dashed toward Max saying, "Papa, Papa!"

Max picked him up and they hugged each other fiercely. "How's my big boy?" Max asked? Finny kept on clinging to his neck, not at all ready to be put down.

The officer was still standing in the doorway, watching and grinning. Jessica asked if she'd like a cup of coffee, but she declined. Both she and Max thanked her several times. Even Finny thanked her by releasing his hold on Max long enough to touch her hand and smile.

✳ ✳ ✳

A week passed. It was a week like weeks should be, a normal one. Jessica found herself smiling all the time, even when dealing with difficult cases. Max was especially busy, but he always found the time to drop by the apartment more often than he ever had before. Cheyenne stayed home with Finny for several days, saying she'd make up her classes later. When everyone was sure Finny's abduction had receded from his memory, he went back to the monastery. The nuns were happy to have him back and assured Jessica over and over that he would be safe. And Jessica's mother was ecstatic over the phone when she heard everything had turned out all right.

Not so with Gunner. Two FBI agents arrived at the Oregon Hospital and Science University and rode the elevator to his office. They knocked and heard a gruff voice yell, "Come in."

They entered. "Are you Dr. Karl Gunner?"

"Of course, I'm Dr. Gunner."

One of the agents stepped toward the desk, flashed his badge and said, "We're the FBI. You're under arrest."

Gunner pushed back from his desk so furiously that his chair tipped over. Standing, he said, "What the hell is this? Arrested for what?"

The other agent said, "For child-trafficking. That is a federal crime."

As he was being handcuffed, Gunner shouted, "No doubt you got information from Antony Scolari. He is out of his mind. Whatever happened out there at that adoption agency—it's called 'Love Me', isn't it?—is entirely his fault. I had nothing to do with it. Mr. Scolari is a liar. He will say anything to try and save his own skin. I need to call my attorney. Now, damn it!"

"You'll get the opportunity to call a lawyer as soon as you're in jail." He was deposited in a police car and taken away.

Dr. Gunner was not seen in the hospital again. He was supposed to be out on bail, but no one Jessica spoke with knew where he was, or even cared. Eventually, she opened her newspaper one morning to discover the case had gone to trial. Then, several weeks after that, she read that Gunner had been found guilty and sentenced to 25 years in prison. Antony was also found guilty, but was only sentenced to 15 years. A whole list of other people have also been found guilty and were going to serve prison sentences.

Early on a Friday morning, Jessica sat in the hospital coffee shop with a cup of coffee and a blueberry muffin reading the newspaper. By now, the trial was over and there was no more news about the scheme, so reporters were doing background pieces. Today's was about the men's experience in the Vietnam War. There were quotes from a psychologist about how being in Vietnam might affect a man's thinking.

Jessica didn't care about how Gunner's mind might have been affected. Her opinion was that he was selfish and conceited, and even evil, not as a result of being in Vietnam but because that was his nature. She was satisfied that Gunner had finally gotten what he deserved. Antony, too, even though he might have been manipulated by Gunner, both during Vietnam and afterwards. Manipulation or not, anybody should know that kidnapping kids is wrong, particularly a man with two kids of his own.

Looking up, she saw Max at her table. He smiled at her and winked. She smiled back and said, "Please sit down."

He did, grasped her hand, and said, "How do you feel this morning?"

"Thanks to you, I feel happy—happy to have you and Finny in my life."

"Me too." He paused and said, "Jessica, the hospital board members apparently had a meeting and voted unanimously to have me replace Gunner."

With a wide-eyed look, she said, "Are you going to take the position?"

"Do you want me too?"

Her brow furrowed. With a soft moan, she said, "I know you would make the best board member, but…" she trailed off.

"Jessica, I'm not interested in recognition, power or control over people. I turned down the opportunity. I really enjoy my practice, and I want to help make our clinic successful. I want to be there when our clinic opens in a month."

Jessica sighed with relief. "You are the greatest man I've ever met." She looked at him intently for a moment and then said, "Would you like to come to Seattle for the Christmas holidays? Mother asked about you, if you could come. She goes overboard with holiday celebrations: food, drinks, company, you name it. She really would like you to be there."

"Of course. I'd love to go with you and Finny to Seattle and spend a few days with your family." His smile sent vibrations throughout her body.

CHAPTER THIRTY- SIX

The forecast for Christmas Eve was for snow. Jessica hoped Christmas would be happy and carefree. She knew her mother would make it extravagant, with lots of gifts.

She and Max were scheduled for surgery that morning. Hers was less complex, so she finished first, picked Finny up from daycare, fed him, and packed for the trip to Seattle.

It was four o'clock in the afternoon, and they were an hour out of Portland. The sun was buried somewhere behind a mass of cumulus clouds sailing overhead, pushed by freezing winds. Max switched on the headlights.

Jessica glanced toward the back seat of the car. Finny was fine, secured in his car seat. She alternately played absently with the buttons on her sweater and rubbed her hands on the side of her slacks as though they were dirty. Finally, she clasped her hands tightly together on her lap.

Max glanced at her and said, "What's bothering you?"

"I'm tired, I guess, and anxious about our visit to Mother's." She wasn't telling him the whole truth. She was always anxious about seeing her mother, so that was honest, but the time had come to tell Max about Finny's father. *If he knew it was Antony,* she thought, *would he discard me like a used coat? Would he want to remain in practice with me? What about our joint ownership in the clinic?*

"You're so quiet. What's wrong, Jessica?" he asked, concern in his voice.

Her head lowered. She couldn't keep it upright. "I need to tell you something." She remained silent for a moment, swallowed hard, and repeated, "I need to tell you something. It's about Finny."

"Does he have a medical problem?" He glanced at her, looking concerned.

"No, no, he's okay."

"Centralia's the next town. Let's stop there. We can stretch our legs, have coffee and talk. Okay?"

Jessica nodded.

They pulled into a roadside restaurant and got coffee and a cup of milk for Finny. Jessica cleared her throat but still couldn't seem to tell Max what needed to be said. She was overcome with embarrassment, guilt, and most of all, the feeling that she had done something wrong. "Max," she said, "you've been so understanding and kind. I need to level with you...."

"Jessica, for heaven's sake, what's going on? Everything's fine." He looked at Finny and said, "Isn't that right?" and the little boy made giggly noises and banged a spoon on the highchair they had put him in.

"OK, Max. You remember Antony, the architect who was involved

218

in child trafficking?" Then it came in a rush, "Antony is Finny's father." Blood drained from her face, but she didn't stop. "It was a one-night stand and I got... Antony didn't know till I told him, and that was after Finny went missing, so that he would tell me where he was sent." She looked at Max, eyes filled with tears. *He'll never see me after this,* she thought. She stood and said, "Please. Let's just go" and headed for the door.

Max paid the bill, picked Finny up, and followed. He got the child back into his car seat and then put his arms around her, held her tightly, and said, "Jessica, it's okay. I still love you and Finny."

"And I love you, too" she replied and then she couldn't say any more.

During the rest of the drive, Jessica felt as though she were suspended in something soft and clingy that didn't let sound, light or feeling in. They approached her mother's home. Max sighed when he saw the size of the property, the entire yard decorated in multicolored lights. Every shrub and fence post was lit. Suspended by thin wires atop Douglas fir trees, angels soared and glowed in the night. They parked, Max pulled Finny from his car seat, and pointed at Rudolf with his red nose. Finny was delighted and Max was laughing.

Jessica started to relax. She couldn't be sure about Max, whether he would want to stay with her and Finny, but for the first time in a long time she felt less worried. She had told him. That was good.

She looked at him now and said with a smile, "Are you ready?"

"Always."

Two taps on the door and it opened, her mother standing there with a smile.

"Merry Christmas, and welcome to our home, Doctor."

"Max will do."

Jessica watched as he entered the house. He moved with confidence and animal grace. How handsome he was, with scattered wisps of gray in his thick unruly head of hair.

Meanwhile, Finny dashed into the house and headed for the kitchen as if guided by Santa himself. He immediately began opening lower cupboards. His grandmother followed him into the kitchen, picked him up, kissed him and gave him a candy cane. Then she asked, "Would you care for a drink, Doctor?"

"Please, call me Max."

Mother appears fascinated with Max, but then again, Mother's always fascinated with men, Jessica thought. She was about to ask a question about her stepfather, when her mother said, "Your stepfather went to Vancouver and won't be back for three days."

Neither Max nor Jessica said anything other than, "I see."

Later that evening, guests arrived, all wearing their Christmas finest. Gorgeous poinsettias sat on every table. Food, beautifully prepared, was everywhere: breads, salads, vegetable trays, desserts. Guests talked and laughed and wished each other a merry holiday. Jessica's mother introduced Max to everyone.

Much later after all the guests had left, Jessica retired to a bedroom with Finny's crib already set up and waiting. Her mother had brought it up from basement storage.

Christmas morning, Jessica looked out the window to see Seattle covered with a blanket of snow. The living room was filled with bright and cheerful Christmas music. She stood by the fireplace, exhaled and rubbed her arms, absorbing the warmth.

Her family tradition dictated that breakfast came first, and then presents could be opened. Her mother had invited several close friends over. Everyone opened gifts, ate, tasted wine, and enjoyed singing songs.

The third day after breakfast, Jessica and Max said thank-you once again, for all the gifts and the wonderful visit, and then they departed for Portland. On the way home, Jessica finally asked, "Do you hate me for what I did, Max? I need your help to unravel the emotional mess I got myself into."

"Oh, Jessica, I don't hate you. I love you. We all make mistakes. Look here, we have this wonderful boy." He turned his head toward Finny, smiled and said, "Right, young man?" Then, he looked at her again and said, "I want you to be happy. I want you to let go of this stress. Let everything fall away. Sing, or do whatever it takes to find a quiet center within yourself. But always keep in mind that I want to be with you."

"Now, I have a favor to ask," Max added. "Be sure you're not working on New Year's Eve. I've made us a reservation at the Ringside Steakhouse for dinner at six o'clock."

On New Year's Eve, Max picked Jessica up at her apartment at half past five. He knocked and then used the key she'd given him, entering with his arms ready for a hug and his lips desirous of a kiss. She welcomed him in kind. She thought he looked very handsome in navy slacks and gray-blue tweed jacket with leather elbows. *And he looks happy, too,* she thought.

She wore a black, wool-rayon sleeveless dress and a satin bolero jacket with three-quarter sleeves. She knew she looked good. Finny was to be with a babysitter, since Cheyenne had gone home for the holidays, so they had the night to themselves. It would be a night to remember.

She smiled and said, "Would you like a glass of wine before we go?"

"Absolutely. Allow me."

He poured the wine and stepped toward her. He slipped his arm around her shoulder, pulled her against him and handed her the glass.

Together they said, "Cheers, and for a great year to come." He kissed her.

"You look gorgeous," he said.

When they arrived at the Ringside Steakhouse restaurant, they were seated near the fireplace. Flames flickered and danced across Jessica's face. Max stared at her for a moment as if daydreaming and finally said, "You're so beautiful."

Jessica felt her cheeks turn warm. Heat seemed to cascade down her neck and across her breasts and arms. She said, "Max, you're the sweetest man ever. I've been fortunate to have met you."

Soon, a scrumptious meal had arrived. They ate, complimented the food, and discussed plans for their clinic, and for providing optimal patient care.

After the meal, Max said, "I'd like you to see our new clinic. It's ready to open the first week in January." He drove her there and showed her every room, leaving her office for last. "This room ends our tour." His smile was wide. "Here it is." He gestured with his hand and she entered her own office.

"What a beautiful office! I love all the windows." She dashed over to a solid cherry desk and stroked its top. There was a photo of Finny on the corner. She picked it up and kissed it. "When did you take this?"

She laughed. "You're so thoughtful." She plopped herself into a leather swivel chair behind the desk and beamed at Max.

"Come, there's more," he said. They stepped into an adjacent, room with two chairs, a round table that held a large bouquet of roses, and an ice bucket that held a bottle of Domain Chandon Brute. Jessica stood there with her mouth open. "When did you find the time to do all this? You're so sweet. It's beautiful."

"Didn't you know I'm a night owl? That's when I do my best work."

He gazed at her as if from afar. Then he knelt on one knee before her, took her hand, and with his other hand pulled from his jacket pocket a tiny, dark blue velvet box. He flipped it open with his thumb, looked up into her eyes and said, "Will you marry me?"

She replied instantly. "Yes. Yes, absolutely."

He stood then and placed the engagement ring on Jessica's finger, embracing and kissing her hard and long. She heard herself purring like a cat. She tilted her head back, and his lips slid to her neck, so smooth. They kissed so passionately that she had to pull back and catch her breath against his warm lips. Her fingers weaved into his hair, and she nuzzled his neck. She was truly happy to be with him.

Max poured the Domain Chandon into two fluted glasses, which they lifted, and together they said, "Cheers and success, and may we have a future filled with happiness."

Max winked at her, kissed her again and added, "And have another child or two for Finny to play and grow up with."